I0658402

Falling Into Knight

A.R. Dean

Falling Into Knight

By A. R. Dean

Published by A R D Publications©

Second Edition

©2013 A. R. DEAN

ISBN-13: 978-0615783772

ALSO BY A.R. DEAN

Bloodline ~ Immersed In You

Bloodline II ~ Daughter of Eve

Falling Into Knight

A.R. Dean

Please be advised that this book contains content of an adult nature and is not suitable for children.

The author acknowledges the copyrighted or trademarked status and trademark owners of the following wordmarks: 50 Shades of Grey; McCarran International Airport; Sylvia Day; Bared to You; Black Parade; Foo Fighters; Walk; UT (University of Texas at Austin); The Bellagio; Velma; Scooby Doo; Fonzy; Happy Days; Hunk Mansion; Fairmont Olympic Hotel; UTMB @ Galveston; Batman; Catwoman; Dark Knight Rises; Southcenter Westfield Mall; Big Bang Theory; Supernatural; The Godfather; Jackie Chan;

Falling Into Knight

A.R. Dean

Acknowledgements

Cover art provided by J. Hill: @ DiversifiedBeat

Table of Contents

ONE

I stood in the middle of the living room surveying the empty apartment. Everything was boxed up and loaded onto the moving van that had left just minutes ago. I would be following shortly but I wanted one last look at the home I'd lived in for the past four and a half years. I loved this place. I was going to miss coming home to it.

I'd moved in my sophomore year of college with my boyfriend Joe. At the time I didn't think I'd live here forever but I did think that wherever I lived it would always be with Joe. Funny how life can take your hopes and dreams and flush them down the toilet.

I'd met Joe my freshman year of school at the ripe old age of twenty-one. It had taken me a little longer to get there. My parents couldn't afford to pay for my schooling, and unfortunately the government said they made too much money for me to qualify for assistance. I was stuck working for a few years trying to save. When I did finally make it, it proved to be worth every penny.

College was awesome. This was a whole new world for me. My entire life I had been pretty sheltered and had not had many friends. As a result I was incredibly shy; so shy that some people thought I was stuck up. I honestly don't know why. I had nothing to be proud or stuck up about. I was an average looking, twenty-one year old girl with long brown hair, big green eyes and a smattering of freckles across my nose. I came from a lower income, working class family, where the kids all had chores to do and we didn't get paid to do them. Living on campus at UT in Austin changed all of that; giving me the opportunity to meet a lot of people; allowing me to break out of my shell.

I had always been thin, too thin, with small boobs and small hips and would have given just about anything to have had a few of the curves my mother was blessed with. Apparently that gene skipped me and went to my sisters. When it came to the gene pool however, I seemed to have collected mine from an unknown source. I didn't look like either of my parents or any of my brothers and sisters.

It was a common joke around the house that I belonged to the milk man, or ice man and sometimes the postman and for a while when I was young I believed it. At least until I met my great aunt Jean on my dad's side of the family. I looked just like her.

But worst of all was my name. Every time I had to write my legal name I groaned and wondered what the hell my mother had been thinking. Drusilla Unity Kosetty...I know – depressing, right? My friends at college called me Ducky at first. Eventually I got them to call me Drew instead. I liked that better, plus it was much easier to type.

Despite my lack of curves, my backwardness, and my weird name I still managed to make a few friends that I hung out with all the way through school. My best friend was Amy. We were both majoring in accounting so we scheduled all of our classes together.

But other than being good in accounting we had no similarities. Where I was shy and backward, Amy was outgoing and friendly. I was strait as a beanpole; Amy was curvy and voluptuous. I had long brown hair; hers was short, spiky and blonde. Amy was bossy and I was...well I wasn't bossy. But no matter, we loved hanging together.

That year had been my year of firsts. My first time to live on my own, my first drink of alcohol, my first time to get smashed, my first real boyfriend with whom I had my first real sex. Joe and I dated that entire first year and the next year decided to move in together.

Amy had tried to talk me out of it but I was so in love with Joe. It didn't matter that he was two years younger than me. I couldn't say no to him about anything, and besides, I really wanted to be with him all the time.

We all finished our degrees at the same time in December, Joe's in mechanical engineering and mine and Amy's in accounting, and we all went to work right away in our respective fields. The bad part was that Amy's job happened to be in Seattle Washington, she was moving back home to be close to her family. I would miss her terribly, but I still had Joe. Things were going great or so it seemed. Then six months ago everything changed.

Joe and I celebrated our one year anniversary of being out of college and holding steady jobs. It just seemed natural that we take our relationship to the next level. After all we loved each other…right? That was what I told myself, and what I told Joe.

Six months ago I told him I wanted more. I wanted to get married and start a family. That was when he told me that I was not the one he wanted to spend the rest of his life with. And just like that my life went down the toilet.

He packed his stuff and moved out that weekend without so much as a backward glance. He got his freedom; I got stuck with the apartment. Not that I couldn't afford it, I made good money but it just wasn't the same without Joe.

I tried to get on with my life but everywhere I turned there was Joe. Joe was at the movies. Joe was at the gas station. And of course Joe was at the only decent happy hour in town. The last straw was when I saw him with another woman. I thought I was going to die, right there in the middle of the grocery store. I left right then; just walked out leaving a shopping cart full of groceries sitting in the middle of the produce section.

I left the store on foot and was halfway home before I realized I'd driven my car to the store. If I'd bought the groceries I probably would have remembered it but somehow it just didn't register. I had to walk all the way back to the store to get it. Luckily, Joe wasn't in the parking lot when I got there.

I called Amy that night and cried into the phone for a full hour. She did her best to comfort me long distance while I bawled and snotted into the mic of my cell phone. Finally, after drinking a bottle of cheap wine and eating an entire box of chocolate covered cherries, I cried myself to sleep.

I woke the next morning with a terrible headache to go along with my stiff back and neck. I had dried drool on my chin, and my face was covered with indentions from sleeping on the carpet. The empty wine bottle and candy box stared at me from under the coffee table, reminding me of the awful night before. I felt like shit. I called in sick, took a shower and went to bed. At noon my phone woke me and when I saw it was Amy I answered.

"I just called your work and they told me you were home sick. How much did you drink last night?"

I really had no idea. "It was just a bottle of cheap wine, I think it was a magnum." Thinking about it made my head hurt worse and I was starting to tear up again.

"Jesus Drew. Listen hon," Amy said, "One of our girls gave her notice today. She is leaving for a better job elsewhere. Her position will be open in a month. I want you to apply. I've already talked to Randy about you and he says if you apply he will call you for an interview. You need to make a clean break."

"I don't know," I said as I rolled the idea around in my head. "I don't know anyone up there." I finished lamely.

18

"You know me and that is all you need to know. Besides, sometimes it's good to go where no-one knows anything about you. You can reinvent yourself. Become whatever you want. Plus this is a great position with great pay and benefits."

"You don't want to stay around there where you see dip-shit all the time. Move up here. You can live with me until you get on your feet and we can catch up. I'm not taking no for an answer. I've already emailed you the app. Fill it out and send it back."

Bossy Amy, always the same I thought. I got off the phone with her and went back to bed. I lay there for half an hour tossing and turning before getting up.

I could feel myself sliding down into a deep, dark pit of depression. It had taken every ounce of energy I could summon, just to make it through the past four months. I couldn't endure another night like last night, not by myself. I needed someone who could hold me together when I started falling apart.

As badly as I wanted to just go to bed and never get out again I knew that wasn't the answer. Life was still moving forward all around me, but I was standing still; stuck in a past that no longer existed for me and Joe. Amy was right, I needed a clean break.

Going to my corner workstation I pulled up my email and printed the application form. After filling it out I pulled up my resume, tweaked it a bit then sent them both to Amy.

I got a call the next day to schedule an interview. I made it for the following Friday then put in a request for vacation and booked a flight. Thursday after work I was on a plane to Seattle. I stayed the night with Amy and had my interview the next day at two. The rest is history.

I take one last look around then leave, locking the door behind me. I stop by the office and turn in my key. I give them my forwarding address so they can mail my deposit refund.

Putting on my sunglasses I turn up the volume on the radio. My iPod is plugged in and Foo Fighters are singing "Walk" as I drive out onto the main highway.

TWO

I occupy a desk in one of thirty cubicles on the fifth floor of Jameson accounting firm. We specialize in corporate accounts and do everything from full service bookkeeping to random audits.

I'm two cubicles down from Amy. A guy name Ned occupies the desk between us. He is somewhat of a geek, although most of the people here are, me included.

I've been introduced to the entire office but I already can't remember the names of half the people. All of them seem really nice though and I think about what Amy said before. I can tell them whatever I want about my life or omit whatever. I can reinvent myself.

I've decided that I am not going to be the poor schmuck who got dumped by her boyfriend and is now struggling to get over him. I'm going to be the hot new kick-ass accountant that moved across country to bravely start a new life. I even went and got a new haircut and a splash of color.

I've never done that one before but it was time for some new firsts. Amy and I started at the day spa this weekend where they pampered, massaged, and waxed our cares away. My dark brown hair now has some deep red low-lights and has been trimmed to just below my shoulder blades with some bangs scissored in.

I look up from my computer screen to see an older man with almost completely gray hair standing next to my cubicle looking at me. He appears to be about five-foot-ten wearing a pair of suit pants with a white shirt and no tie. His gray eyes sparkle at me as the skin around his eyes and mouth crinkle into a smile.

Extending a hand to me he introduces himself. "Hello, I hear that you are the new girl who is taking Pamela's place. Nice to meet you, I'm Larry."

"Yes, that's right. I'm Drew, So nice to meet you Larry." I have no idea who Larry is but he seems nice, and his smile is genuine.

"Welcome to the company." He says cupping my hand between his two.

"Thank you." I reply.

All around me people are walking by or sticking their head out of their cubicle to say hi to

Larry. Somehow I get the feeling I should know who he is. I can tell that he is well liked by everyone and he seems to like everyone in return.

When he'd gone I grabbed Amy. "Who was that?" I asked.

Amy grinned. "That was Larry Jameson. This is his company."

She must have seen the look of shock on my face. "Everyone reacts the same way when they find out. He's just a real nice man and people love working for him. You'd never know he owned the place by the way he acts."

At lunch time Amy grabs me to go to the break room. We've ordered from a local deli and its waiting for us. She wants to introduce me to some of the upper management along the way.

The break room is on the sixth floor so we swing into the stairwell and take a quick flight up. Right now I'm wishing I had worn flats instead of the stiletto pumps but being my first day I wanted to look my best.

Amy keeps telling me how good I look and I must admit it goes a long way to boost my morale. I actually feel pretty today. Something I haven't felt in – well six months.

We stop by Randy's office and say hello. I know Randy because he interviewed me. He is a tall, very thin, blond haired man with pale blue eyes, wire framed glasses and a pocket protector in his shirt pocket. Standing next to him I realize I'm as tall as he is in my stilettos but he appears much taller. I guess because he is so thin.

She introduces me to Connie next. Amy tells me what department she is over but I'm trying to pay attention to what Connie is saying to me. She is a very boisterous woman with an annoying voice that grates on my nerves and I'm glad my desk is not close to hers. She must be fifty inches around the bust and is shaped like an ice cream cone. She's wearing a peach colored pleated skirt that is the wrong thing to wear below her raglan sweater and I'm reminded of Velma from Scooby Doo.

As she leads me around the corner Amy leans over and whispers, "Just wait till you meet Adam," in my ear. I don't have time to ask who Adam is because she is pulling me into the next office. We stop in front of a desk with a bronze name plate that reads Adam Knight. At the moment he has his back to us typing something on his computer. Amy clears her throat.

"Be with you in just a sec." He says in a very deep, ultra sexy voice.

I take in his hair peeking over the back of his chair; dark chestnut brown with curls. That's all I can see from this angle. And then he turns around.

OMG – WOW - he is – holy mother of god – he is HOT!

How do you say Adonis; perfection in the form of a man? That chestnut brown hair was just the tip of the iceberg. It had just enough loose curl to add some body and definition. Just add a dab of gel, run fingers through - et voila! And that is exactly what it looked like he'd done.

His eyes are a deep shade of blue, bordering on violet, perfectly framed by thick black lashes and eyebrows. His lips are well defined, the lower one full beneath a nicely shaped nose. He is clean shaven but the shadow of facial hair is evident just below the surface.

He smiles revealing even, white teeth and a deep dimple in his right cheek. My eyes travel to his chest taking in the taut, white dress shirt that can't hide the broad shoulders or the guns he has for arms.

I stand there gawking for a moment before my subconscious elbows me in the gut and tells me to snap out of it. *Remember you're supposed to be the hot, kick-ass accountant, not the dribbler.* I snap my mouth shut and step forward extending my hand to him in the most professional way I can muster.

"Adam, this is Drew. She's taking Pamela's place." Amy says introducing me. "Drew, this is Adam Knight.

Adam sits there smiling for a minute then suddenly realizes that I'm holding out my hand. He jumps up out of his seat abruptly reaching forward and knocks over his cup of coffee.

Amy runs around the corner to the break room for paper towels while Adam tries to contain the mess, cursing under his breath. The hot liquid is quickly spreading across the entire surface and I grab up the stapler and tape dispenser just in time, hoping it doesn't reach the edge.

Amy is back in moments and I take a stack of napkins from her working on one side of the desk while she mops up the other side preventing the hot, brown liquid from spilling onto the cream colored carpet. When the mess is finally cleaned up; sodden napkins raked into the trash can, Adam leans over and shakes my hand. I notice the long fingers and clean, manicured nails. This guy is too good to be true.

"So sorry about that," he says looking highly embarrassed and flashing a thousand megawatt smile. The man is so damn dreamy and now standing before me I can see the whole package. Flat abs and narrow hips that make the pleated front pants he is wearing look awesome.

"Not a problem." I smile back. *I'll come clean up your coffee anytime!*

We leave Adam's office and head straight to the break room. As soon as we are out of earshot I lean in to Amy.

"So tell me about Adam." Amy glances around the break room.

"Not here." She whispers back. "Let's go up to the roof top."

"Okay, I agree, but can we take the elevator?"

We pick up our lunches and Amy steers me down the hall to the bank of elevators. A minute later we step out onto the gorgeous sunlit roof top. A gentle breeze teases a loose strand of hair pulling it out of my ponytail. There are several umbrella covered tables up here and we choose a spot close to the railing. No one else is out on the roof today so we can talk without being overheard.

"So you think he's hot?" Amy asked wagging her eyebrows at me.

"Definitely, is he married? Engaged, Girlfriend?"

"Nope, nope and nope."

"Really, that surprises me, Why not?"

"I'm not sure exactly, but I have a theory. I think he's just incredibly shy. Pretty women intimidate him and things happen. Like coffee getting spilled etc… Anyway my guess is when girls first see him they go all crazy on him and scare him to death. Then every time they're around him he comes across as a klutz. At least that's my theory."

"He doesn't look like a klutz."

"Nope but he did knock his coffee over so I'll bet he thinks you're hot too."

I laugh. "That's nice to know."

"Maybe you can un-klut-ze-tize him and make him your own."

"Nice Amy, but I'm not ready for my own yet."

"Ducky, it's been six months now, time to move on."

"I am moving on and please don't call me that. I'm just not ready to move on with someone else... just yet."

"No one said you had to have a relationship either, how about a distraction?"

"Yea maybe, I'm not even sure about that right now."

"So why did you want info on him."

Grinning wickedly I leaned over and whispered, "Because it gives me more to fantasize with when I have to pull out B.O.B."

Amy howled with laughter, almost choking on her cherry coke. "Sorry, guess I should have painted you a better picture."

"What about you Amy? You're not interested?" I asked, realizing I'd not seen or heard about Matt since I'd been here. Matt was, or is Amy's on again - off again boyfriend of the last two and a half years and I was surprised that he'd not been around.

Amy frowned. "No, at the moment I'm just not interested in any kind of relationship. I spent so much time waiting on Matt that I feel like I missed out on life."

"So what happened with Matt? I was halfway expecting to be living with him too when I moved up here."

"We were talking of him moving in with me and then he got all flaky on me. I told him to forget it. I think after this long you should know whether or not you want to be with someone. Since he didn't, I made the decision for him.

I was ready to get on with my life. He wasn't ready to be part of that so I told him goodbye. Honestly, I feel good about my decision."

The next three weeks are pretty uneventful. I see Adam around and he always smiles politely and nods to acknowledge me but never approaches for conversation. A few times it seems he wants to say something to me, but I don't encourage him. I just try to keep my distance. Ned has asked me out a couple of times but I always decline. Don't get me wrong, he seems like a nice guy, just not my type and I don't want to lead him on.

I've gotten two paychecks now and am well on my way to having my own apartment. Not that Amy wants me out or anything, but eventually I'll want my own space and she'll want hers back. I set a goal for January of next year. That will give me six months.

This week I want to get a membership at the local gym and also to buy some new clothes. It seems that I've lost some weight these last few months and a lot of my things are now way too big. Friday we have plans to go out after work with some of the people from the office. I'm excited about going. It will be good for me to get to know my co-workers better and it's been too long since I've gone out and enjoyed myself.

Wednesday evening, after my shower Amy comes into my room to check out what I'm planning to wear Friday night. I'm rummaging through the last of my boxes, pulling stuff out and putting it away. Most of my stuff is in storage. I brought only clothes and things I couldn't live without to Amy's.

"Damn girl, you're skinnier than you were in college. I wish I had that problem."

I'm disappointed. "These are the smallest pair of jeans I own and they are too big now." I say as I fall back onto the bed.

"Let's go to the mall tomorrow after work and get some stuff. I could use a new pair of jeans too."

"Okay," I agree. "I haven't seen the mall yet."

"I'll take you to Southcenter. We can stop and have dinner and make it a night if you want. As long as I'm in bed by ten I'm okay."

"That sounds good; maybe I can find a few outfits for work too. I was hoping to go shopping on Saturday anyway."

"It's a plan then."

We sit in the living room and eat pizza out of a cardboard box, drinking a few beers while watching reality TV. It's not my thing but I get a kick out of how excited Amy gets over the stuff, plus there are some really cute guys to drool over.

I call my mom later before I go to bed. This is the first time I've spoken with her since before I left. I had waited till the last minute to tell her I was leaving; just knowing she was going to be upset. I had been shocked when she wasn't. Instead she had been understanding and supportive, telling me that I was still young and single and to enjoy being able to travel, just make sure I kept in touch and went to visit her once in a while. I was so glad for her reassurance. After that I knew everything was going to be alright.

At lunch the next day I walk a few blocks over to the gym and sign up. I want to be able to work out Saturday and it will be easier to get this part out of the way now. I've already called ahead and Jim, one of the sales associates is expecting me. The sky is threatening to rain when I leave. I hope it doesn't because I forgot my umbrella in my desk. I take a quick tour of the gym then head back to work, wolfing down a sandwich before returning to my desk.

Amy and I leave immediately after work to go to the mall. I've brought a pair of flats to wear and change into them in the car. We arrive at the Westfield Southcenter Mall and immediately I get the feeling I'm going to love this place. Grabbing a bite to eat first, we hit the stores. It doesn't take me long to decide I do love this place. It has all of my favorite stores plus a few I'd never heard of. We shop until the mall is about to close then head home. I've spent way too much money but I have some very nice, new clothes that fit perfectly. My favorites are the jeans and top I bought for tomorrow night. I also caught a shoe sale and got a new pair of stilettos. Tomorrow night I'll be ready to hit the town.

THREE

We chose a small, local pub to meet where we could eat and play a few games. There would also be a band starting at nine-thirty. Our group occupied a section that was made up of two long tables pushed together. Ned and a couple of the guys had come early to secure the spot for us. Amy and I had gone back to the apartment to shower and dress.

"Hon, you are smokin' hot!" Amy had said as I walked out of my room. I smiled; pleased with the way I looked in my new jeans and halter top. "Are you ready to get your wobble on?"

I laughed, remembering how Amy and I used to dance. The girl had some serious moves to go with her curves. I tried to copy her but somehow I just couldn't do it justice. "I'm ready." I said taking a final look in the mirror, checking my make-up.

Tonight, in keeping with the whole re-invention idea, I decided to try for the sultry look. I did my eyes with a smoky charcoal and used a slightly darker lipstick than normal. I even used a little blush. My hair I pulled straight back in a sleek ponytail, wrapped a strand of hair around the band and styled my bangs.

Grabbing my purse I checked for my keys and cell phone. Satisfied that I had everything I needed, we headed out the door for the waiting cab. We wouldn't be driving tonight.

It was still early when we arrived; some of our group would not be coming until the band started. Amy and I both ordered a burger and ate while listening to Ned and Jason's playful banter. By the time we finished six more of our group had arrived. I ordered a beer and Amy got a margarita.

Connie came in just as we started our first drink. I was surprised. I hadn't expected any of the management team to show up. She was her normal boisterous self and her voice carried over the din that was starting to build. I noticed she was wearing another pleated skirt. Someone really needed to talk to her about her fashion sense. The skirt would have been alright, just not on her. It hit her just below the knees revealing her over-developed calf muscles and her two inch black pumps.

Ned and Jason had started playing a game of pool, so a group of us gather around to watch. A waitress came around taking orders and I got a second beer and drank it leaning against a low bar by the pool table.

It was nine thirty now and the band was starting to play. I was about to return to the table when I felt someone's eyes drilling holes into my back. I turned around, scanning the room when I saw him leaning on one elbow at the bar across the room. It was Adam.

He caught my eye and smiled that thousand megawatt smile of his, showing off that beautiful dimple. I smiled back. The man was even more gorgeous in jeans and pullover than he was in the dress slacks – if that were possible.

He stood and started across the room toward me. My breath hitched in my throat. Despite what I'd told myself and Amy, I was very attracted to him. Part of me really wanted him to come over and talk to me but the other part was scared. The memory of Joe walking out the door was still too fresh on my mind. It had only been seven months. I still felt a jolt of pain when I thought of it.

My heart was racing now. I needed to leave but he knew I'd seen him and that would just be rude. Not to mention, not a good move since he was technically one of my bosses. True he wasn't over my department, but he was upper management.

I mentally tried to steel myself. He was still heading right for me. Then Connie stepped in front of him, drawing his attention and essentially blocking his view. I owed her one. Maybe I wouldn't be quite so unkind when it came to her clothing. I was safe for the moment. Quickly I found Amy and made my way to the dance floor.

I made it a point to stay as far away from him as possible for the rest of the night. Only one other time did I see him attempt to approach me. I knew if he did I would cave. He was just too good looking and I was just too ready to forget my painful breakup - a bad combination. Still I stood rooted in place as he weaved his way through the crowd toward me. Then a hand was on my arm pulling me out onto the dance floor again. It was Ned.

Never before had I felt such relief and such loss at the same time. My eyes scanned the crowd for signs of Adam. Finally they landed on his broad shoulders as he walked out the front door.

Adam rolled over in bed. Rubbing the sleep from his eyes, he glanced at the clock. "Shit," he exclaimed shooting out of bed. It was already nine a.m. and he was supposed to meet Davy at the gym in a half hour for a game of one on one.

Adam had met Davy ten years ago when he was working at Dominic's Italian restaurant part time while he went to school. A transplant from Brooklyn, Davy had come into the restaurant looking for work. They'd hired him on as a cook and the two had become fast friends.

Despite the fact he'd been in Seattle now for ten years, Davy still had his Brooklyn accent and his bad boy mannerism. Adam had been sure there were no other Italians in Seattle quite like Davy until the day he showed up at his apartment with Gloria.

Adam had never known that two people could be so much alike but Davy and Gloria were two peas in a pod. Gloria was a nice person but she often said what she thought without incorporating her brain to mouth filter. She was a pretty woman with mid-back length, bottle red hair that she kept permed in tight curls. She wore said hair big most of the time and always adorned with a scarf, usually a colorful one.

Her make-up was a bit gaudy with vibrant hues of eye shadow, false lashes and deep red lipstick – all piled on thick. She looked good though, there was no denying that. You would never catch her out of sorts. She was always dressed to kill even if just working around the house.

Quickly, Adam pulled on some jog pants, a tee-shirt and a ball cap on backwards to cover his bed head. He would shower and comb his hair after the game. Right now he didn't have time for it.

As he drove to the gym, his mind wandered back to the night before and his unsuccessful attempts to talk to Drew. He had never had a problem talking to women in general. He dealt with them on a daily basis at work and had dated his fair share of them over the years. But for some reason the more he was attracted to them, the more nervous he was around them. It was for this reason that the majority of the women he dated were just friends.

Drew wasn't one of the "*just friends*" type. She was incredibly attractive and she definitely made him nervous - in all the right ways. He could feel his heart beating out of his chest every time she looked at him. His mouth went dry and his palms sweaty, but something about her called to him on a baser level. Despite his fears of doing or saying the wrong thing he knew he had to talk to her. This was the one girl he wouldn't be able to stay away from.

The trouble was he didn't really know how to approach her. He'd made more than one trek around the pub last night trying to talk to her and she just seemed to be avoiding him. In the end, he gave up and went home. He needed a new strategy. He needed to talk to Davy.

Arriving at the gym he met Davy on the basketball court. Davy greeted him with a slap on the back and a toothy grin.

"So how did your night out go? You score?" Davy had started dribbling the ball, bending low. Adam took the same stance opposite him, his arms outstretched as he watched Davy's every move.

"No such luck." Adam said frowning.

"You mean you didn't see no-one there that floated your boat?"

Adam shook his head. "Actually I did, but I never got to talk to her. I was hoping you could help me out and give me some pointers."

Davy eyed him incredulously, one eyebrow arched, "pointers…for you…about a girl?" Davy sounded doubtful. "What kind of pointers?"

"It's a girl from work. I've been watching her for weeks now, trying to get up the nerve to go talk to her. I just didn't know what to say to start a conversation with her. I needed something to break the ice. Last night I finally got up the nerve, but every time I tried, someone would grab her to dance or want to talk to me about something. I couldn't seem to get near her. "

Davy stopped dribbling the ball and stood speechless for a minute with a puzzled look on his face. "Whad'ya mean you don't know what to say? Just say whatever pops into your head."

"I don't know about that. If you saw me when she gets close by; my heart starts racing and my vision gets all blurry. Sometimes I think my brain isn't getting enough oxygen. No telling what I'll say when I get like that."

"Actually that is a common problem," Davy says smiling. "It's called thinking with your dick and it usually causes a person trouble."

"I'm being serious here," Adam said, rolling his eyes.

"Me too," said Davy as he feigned left then took a shot overhead. It hit the rim and Adam caught it on the rebound sinking it for a score.

"So," Davy said, "I've never seen you have a problem talking to a girl before. You've been out with lots of girls. What's the problem with this one?"

"The problem is this one is very attractive, and it's the attractive ones that I can't seem to talk to without making a mess of it. Hell the first time I met her I practically dumped a cup of coffee on her, and then she wound up cleaning it up."

"Sounds like a great girl." Davy said laughing. "So what you're saying is, the girls you've been going out with, you're not attracted to?" It was more of a question than a statement.

Adam nodded. "Pretty much, I mean they're nice and all but…"

"…Not who you see yourself spending the rest of your life with." Davy finished his sentence for him.

Adam nodded again, "Exactly!"

Davy shook his head in disbelief. Again he stopped dribbling the ball, this time placing it under his arm. He stood staring at Adam as if seeing him for the first time. The two of them had been friends for too long for Davy to not know something this important.

"I just can't believe that." He said shaking his head. "So why did you bother going out with 'em if you weren't really in to 'em?"

Adam shrugged his shoulders. "I don't know. Maybe I thought I might really like them if I got to know them better. And part of me thinks that a girl like Drew…well what would she want with a guy like me. You know what I mean?"

"No, I don't know what you mean. What the hell are you talking about? I'm telling ya, you are one nice looking son-of-a–bitch and you are a good person too. There's not a girl out there that wouldn't give her eye-teeth to be with you. Everywhere you go girls are vying for your attention."

"I don't know Davy." Adam said, resting his hands on his knees.

"What do ya mean you don't know? He stepped a little closer. "The fact is, there's a girl right now, been sitting out there on the bleachers just watching you."

"Really?" Adam stood up straight stretching his back and shoulders.

"Yea, but don't look now. Wait till ya don't have to turn your head to see her." Davy grinned shaking his head. "Man o' man is she a looker too. She's sitting there in that tight little getup, drinking her little bottle of water, wiping that sweat off her neck, Um-um-um."

44

A slow grin spread across Adam's face. "You're shittin' me aren't you? Trying to get me to look, there's no one there is there?"

Davy smiled back. "Oh she's there alright." Then thrusting the ball in to Adam's chest he said, "Now let's show her whacha got."

Adam took off down the court with Davy blocking him at every turn. Finally he found an opening, cut around Davy and took his shot, banking the ball off the backboard straight into the net. As the ball slipped through he gave a small fist pump then turned back down the court at a trot, scanning the bleachers as he went.

The instant he saw her he stopped. It was Drew. She was leaving and he only saw her face for a minute but he was sure it was her. Had she known it was him? He wished he'd looked up sooner. It might have given him the chance to finally talk to her but it was too late now. He stood transfixed, staring after her until he could no longer see her.

Davy stopped next to him, his eyes tracking in the direction that Adam stood staring.

"It's her," Adam said, "the girl from work."

"Why didn't ya go say hi?"

Adam shrugged his shoulders. "She was already leaving."

Davy shook his head grinning. "Man you do got it bad. Tell you what; come by the house with me. G- has some books that'll give you some ideas about what to say to her. She won't mind ya borrowing them for a while. She's already read 'em like ten times"

Adam nodded. He could use all the help he could get.

Pulling up in the drive behind Davy, Adam parked his car and got out then followed him into the house. The aromas of homemade meat sauce and garlic hit his nose instantly causing his stomach to growl.

"Ay, G- I'm home now. I brought Adam with me. Can you fix us something to eat?" He yelled as he walked thought the front door.

"I'll be right there. I'm trying to put my eyes on." She yelled from somewhere in the back.

Davy walked into the bedroom still yelling. "Ay, I told Adam he could borrow a couple of your books. He needs some ideas about talkin' to a girl."

"Okay, that's fine," came the yelled reply.

Davy walked out of the room with a stack of books under his arm and carried them to the breakfast bar, motioning for Adam to follow.

He began laying the books out on the counter as Gloria came into the room. She walked up to Adam and gave him a huge hug and planted her red lips on the side of his face leaving an imprint on his cheek.

"Hello handsome, I haven't seen you in a while. You been eatin'? It don't look like you're eatin' good" She said shaking her head and patting Adam on the belly. Her enormous hoop earrings swung back and forth.

"Hey G-, I know it's been a while, I've just been working a lot."

Davy held up one of the books. "Now this one," he said holding it for Adam to see, "this one here's got some good stuff in it." He said with a chuckle, raising his eyebrows.

Gloria looked at the book then back at Adam, a slow smile spreading across her face. "What's the matter with you Adam?" She asked as she smacked her gum in a very pronounced manner. "You need somethin' to help put some sticka in your pecka?"

Adam blushed.

"Gloria, you can't be saying stuff like that to my friend. You're gonna give him a heart attack."

Frowning, Adam took the book from Davy, noting the book was clearly a novel. "I thought you were giving me some self-help books. What am I going do with a novel?"

"Read 'em," Davy replied, "and take good notes. If you wanna know what women these days wanna hear, you can find it in these books."

"You've read these?" Adam asked skeptically, one eyebrow raised.

"Only the dirty parts," Gloria interjected.

Davy shot her a dirty look. "Now why the hell you wanna tell my friend that?" He asked.

"Because it's the truth," she replied tartly.

Adam read the title of the first book, "50 Shades of Grey", the second book "Bared to you" and three other titles. He'd never heard of any of them.

He gathered the books up under his arm. "Okay, I'll take a look at them." He said.

"Oh, don't carry those out there like that. Let me get you a bag to put them in. You don't want anyone to see you with those books."

"Why not?"

Davy grinned. "Anyone sees you with those books you really will have a hard time gettin' a girl. Everyone will think you're gay."

Gloria slapped Davy on the shoulder with a loud whack.

"Great," Adam said, "that's just what I need."

FOUR

I woke up Saturday morning with only small hangover, thankful that I was feeling better than I deserved. Making myself a cup of coffee I took an ibuprofen and headed for the shower. I'd gotten in late last night and went straight to bed. Not only was my hair a mess but I had raccoon eyes and I felt sticky.

I showered quickly and dressed in my workout suit. I'd need another shower later but for now I felt one hundred percent better. Filling my water bottle I grabbed a gym towel and headed out the door.

The gym was practically empty so I had my pick of machines. The treadmills were all on the second floor. I made my way up the stairs and chose a machine way down at the end, overlooking the basketball courts. Putting in my earphones I turned on my iPod and started walking, warming up with My Chemical Romance's *The Black Parade*.

It took only a few minutes for me to get warmed up and I increased my speed to a steady jog.

I loved running. I had started as a kid in school doing the cross country and hadn't stopped since. I always felt good after a run and it didn't hurt my legs any either. The one body part I had that I actually felt good about was my legs. The running kept them trimmed and toned. I was five miles into it, when I happened to look over into the basketball court. A couple of guys were playing now.

Sweating profusely and almost out of water, I needed a refill and a cool down before I left. I slowed my pace to a walk for another five minutes then got off the machine. The water fountain was downstairs next to the mini bleachers that looked into the courts. I made my way downstairs, refilled my bottle and planted myself on the second row of the bleachers. I'd always like watching sports so I settled for a few minutes drinking my water and watching the guys play.

There was something familiar about one of the men. My eyes widened in surprise when he turned his face toward me and I realized it was Adam. In his cutout tee I could clearly see his awesomely muscled arms and even part of his ribcage. I sat transfixed, watching his every move.

He was so graceful out there on the court; so deliberate and decisive; I just couldn't see him being shy like Amy had suggested. His jog pants were soaked with sweat and were clinging to his thighs. Just watching him I felt my heart rate going up again.

The other guy with him looked my way during a break in the game, saying something to Adam. I tensed. I hoped Adam wouldn't turn around and find me lusting after him. I needed to leave but I couldn't seem to peel my eyes away. He was bending over now with his hands on his knees. Damn he had a nice bum!

Drinking the last of my water, I wiped the sweat from my face and neck then got up to leave. I wasn't ready for anyone in my life I told myself again for the hundredth time since the day I'd met Adam Knight.

Adam dumped the contents from the cardboard Chinese carry out box into his bowl. Grabbing a beer he carried his food into the living room to watch TV while he ate.

Choosing to sit on the floor in front of the couch he stretched his legs out under the coffee table and ate while he flipped through the TV channels.

There was nothing on tonight that he cared to watch so he flipped through his recordings, deciding on a re-run of Supernatural.

He hated nights like this; dinner alone, sitting on the floor watching crap television. He was thirty years old now and tired of spending every night just like this one. He wanted someone that he could share his time with, eat dinner with then wake up and have breakfast too. He was ready to find a girl and settle down.

As he stared at the TV screen, not really seeing, he made a mental list of the girls he'd dated in the past year. There had really only been a few, but most of them he'd gone out with only one time. Why had he bothered dating girls he was not attracted to?

He closed his eyes. Maybe because the one that he had been physically attracted to, had been rude and demanding. She'd had no qualms about telling him how inadequate he was, which only served to make him tense and uncomfortable. He had felt judged at every turn. They didn't date long.

Distractedly, he stabbed at a piece of pork with his chopstick. Drew was different. She was genuinely nice to everyone. He'd seen her interact with her co-workers and everyone seemed to like her. He didn't miss the looks the other men gave her either as she walked by. The thought of her being with someone else got under his skin in an irritating sort of way. It was not a thought he wanted to entertain. He needed to find a way to talk to her soon.

Getting up, he rinsed his bowl and was putting it in the dishwasher when he noticed the paper bag on the counter. Opening the bag he dumped the contents out.

It took him a few minutes to figure out the five books. They were sets, so if he was going to read one of them it should be the first of the set. After reading the backs of the books he decided on *Bared to You, by Sylvia Day.*

Settling into his recliner he opened the book and started reading. It wasn't too bad at first, but after just a few chapters he was starting to understand why people used E-readers…so that no-one could see what you were reading. He caught himself blushing a few times; looking around to make sure he was truly alone. Another few pages and he was hooked.

"OMG…" He stopped reading. Did he just say that out loud? Davy was right. People would think he was gay. But he sure felt anything but gay right now. In his mind he was creating his own version of the characters and the girl looked just like Drew. Of course he would be Gideon. Damn…could he be

Gideon? He wasn't sure if he had that kind of stamina. He smiled to himself. He could try and find out.

Reading this book though, and thinking about Drew, there was no doubt in his mind about whether or not he could get it up. He was going to have to relieve himself at some point or have blue balls. *No wonder Davy read this! But Gloria was probably right; he probably just skipped around to the sex scenes...*

It amazed him that a book with a cover this benign could have so much sex inside. Too bad it didn't have pictures too. He closed his eyes for a minute trying to focus. He was supposed to be getting ideas about what to say to Drew. So far he only had ideas about what he wanted to do to her.

Determined he pushed on through three more chapters. He was squirming in his seat now. *Did Drew wax? Wow, that would be hot. Davy said he should take notes. Could he really say some of this stuff to a girl? It was really sexy in the book but in real life? Suppose she filed sexual harassment on him!!!*

He read another paragraph. *Oh shit - this is intense!* He wondered if Gideon had to go finish up in the bathroom like he was about to do. Getting out of the recliner he was so stiff it hurt. Taking a moment he rearranged himself, and then limped off down the hall. He couldn't take much more of this reading. It was suddenly clear to him why some women went to bed with a good book.

As he entered the bathroom he stopped in front of the mirror studying his reflection. Davy had said he was a good looking guy. Did Drew think he was attractive?

He set the book down and turned the hot water on in the shower then picked it up reading that last paragraph again. Davy had said this was what women wanted to hear. He didn't know if it was true or not but it sure got him going.

Tuesday, the following week, I ran into Adam in the break room as I was getting my lunch.

"Hi Drew." He said. "I saw you at the gym this weekend." I blushed. *Did he see me drooling after him?* "I didn't know you worked-out there. Do you go often?"

"That was actually my first time." I managed to say. I was totally unprepared to talk to him. He was just standing there looking all yummy and I could feel my heart racing in my chest again. Any minute I would probably start sweating. Why did he have this effect on me? I'd been around a lot of nice looking guys before and none of them had me so worked up. But I know it's because I'm attracted to him despite the fact I say I shouldn't be. No matter what I try to tell myself my body betrays me every time I come into contact with this man.

He looks as if he's about to say something else when Amy comes in. "You ready?" She asks.

I nod and we leave together for the roof. I can't help but notice how disappointed Adam looks; for some reason that makes me feel good...

FIVE

I wake up Monday morning just knowing that this is going to be a hell of a day. Monday normally is anyway just by virtue of being Monday, but today is going to be much worse.

Don't ask me how I know. Maybe it's because of all the dreams I had about Joe that had caused me to wake in the middle of the night, after which I had been unable to go back to sleep. Maybe because when I did finally get back to sleep, I slept right through my alarm clock. Maybe it was because when Amy woke me up I had only twenty minutes to get dressed and out the door, or the fact that I had a headache and no time for a cup of coffee.

Whatever it was, it was only exacerbated by the fact that I broke my heel on the step as I ran down the stairs and had to go all the way back up to change my shoes. Then I couldn't find the pair I needed and when I did find them I hit my head on the counter they were sitting under.

I was late to work and had to hunt for a parking spot. By the time I made it to my desk my head was pounding and I was wishing I'd called in sick.

To make matters worse Randy re-assigned me to another account. He apologized profusely but stated I was the best person for the job since my experience with small business was recent. It was for a good friend of his that needed help with his start-up company books.

Even though I had a ton of work to do I couldn't get into it. My mind kept returning to the dreams from the night before. Thoughts of Joe kept emerging from the shallow grave I'd buried them in. I wanted to put my head down on my desk and cry. Could this day get any worse? *Damn him; damn him to hell for doing this to me!*

As the day progressed my frazzled morning morphed into a disastrous mid-morning. I worked through my first break and was an hour late for my lunch break when my phone rang. I answered it without looking at the caller ID only for my disastrous day to suddenly get much worse. My back stiffened when I heard the voice on the other end of the line. It was Joe.

"Hey Drew, I went by the apartment last night to see you and they told me you'd moved. Where are you?"

I couldn't believe he had the nerve to call me after everything he had done to me; after months of no contact at all, I just couldn't process it. Suddenly hearing his voice on the other end of the line had my emotions going a hundred different directions, but to make matters worse, everything I'd ever wanted to say to him since the day he'd left was stuck in my throat.

I wanted so badly to tell him to "piss off" or something to show him that I was moving on and didn't have time for him, but my new-found self-confidence had apparently gone on vacation. My new and improved self-image just up and walked out on me. Each time I opened my mouth nothing would come out, not even a croak, and Joe just kept right on talking like we were best buddies again.

Thank god Amy happened to walk by just then and, seeing the expression on my face, reached over and took the phone away from me. It took her all of ten seconds to tell Joe what a piece-of-shit-dirt-bag he was and that I didn't want to talk to him or see him ever again. She told him not to bother calling and interfering with my life anymore. Then she abruptly ended the call.

I was out of my chair, fairly running to the bathroom; tears escaping despite my attempts to hold them at bay. Amy was right behind me, giving me a shoulder to cry on and holding a box of tissue for me while I tried to pull myself together.

"Have you gone to lunch yet?" Amy asked me as I splashed some water on my face, thankful I was wearing waterproof mascara.

"Not yet." I managed through broken breaths. "This day really sucks."

"I'm sorry hon," Amy was saying. "I know you've had a bad morning. Tonight we're getting you a new phone and a new number. Then we'll stop and pick-up a bottle of wine or two."

"You need to take a break for now though. Go eat, clear your head and when you get back you'll be more relaxed. Nothing here is so important that you stay tied up in knots over it."

She was right. I needed a break. I would go sit on the roof and eat and enjoy the sunshine for a while, if there was any sunshine, as soon as I was able to stop crying.

Amy leaned against the counter as I wiped at my eyes. She glanced at my old phone and wrinkled her nose. "It's about time you got rid of The Beast anyway." She said shaking her head. "I can't believe you still have it."

She was referring to my über-old flip phone that I'd had forever. The thing was damn near indestructible and was almost an extension of my body. I could T9 on that phone faster than most could type on a smart phone. But lately it got too hot to hold up to my ear for more than a minute.

I shrugged my shoulders. "It's been dependable. But it is time for a new one. I guess I'm going to upgrade to the hi-tech world and get that smart phone I've been looking at."

Amy brought my purse to me and left me alone to pull myself together. Ten minutes of cold water, eye drops and concealer later I looked almost normal again.

The call from Joe had seriously rattled me. I felt like an idiot that I couldn't even tell him where to get off. Despite the fact that I kept telling myself I didn't need anyone else in my life, I suddenly realized that really I'd been waiting for Joe to come back.

I was pathetic. The phone call today forced me to see just how stupid I was. He had hurt me so badly when he walked out but I was making things worse by hanging on to false hope.

His call out of the blue seemed to rattle some semblance of sense into me. I had sat around pining and crying for eight months, praying that Joe would tell me he wanted me back. I had been depressed and miserable, refusing to get out with other people, using *I wasn't ready* as an excuse.

The phone call had been a light from heaven, miraculously opening my unseeing eyes. People don't love someone and walk away without a word, then pop up months later expecting everything to continue as it was before.

It was a revelation. Joe didn't love me then. Even if he came back to me I could never expect more than what he'd given me before…and that was not enough. I had wanted more. That was what had sent him over the edge in the first place. I wanted more. More than what he could give – at least to me.

For the first time in eight months something in my brain snapped into place; something that had been badly off. It didn't make the pain go away instantly, but the feeling of despair was gone and I suddenly knew I was going to be alright; alright in a world without Joe. I was free to move on with my life.

Pushing away from the bathroom counter I check my hair once again, square my shoulders and walk back out into the office. As I near the bank of elevators I change my mind about eating what I've brought for lunch. I think instead I want to walk down to the corner bistro. I need to get out of the building for a while.

I hit the down button and almost immediately it dings for me. I step into the elevator and look up as the door closes behind me. One other person occupies the car. It's Adam.

He looks at me curiously, with a touch of concern. "Are you ill?" He asks looking at his watch. "It's early to be going home.

"No," I wave my hand dismissively, "Just a late lunch."

"Oh," he looks relieved, "Me too."

He gives me a sideways glance as if contemplating a question, while his fingers tap out the theme for the Lone Ranger on the elevator wall behind his back. I'm suddenly very uncomfortable being in the small confines of the elevator with him. Everything about him is so sexy and arousing. I can feel my face flushing just thinking about it and avert my eyes to the floor. *Damn, he even has sexy shoes!*

I look back up at him through my lashes. His expression is instantly filled with resolve. A split second decision and he is suddenly moving across the open space of the car to the control panel. He presses the emergency stop button, bringing the elevator to an abrupt halt. My eyes are wide with surprise as he turns toward me, backing me into the corner.

He's so close I can smell his body-wash. I can feel the heat radiating off his body as he leans toward me. Then he kisses me and I melt into him. Surely this is not someone that has trouble being around women.

Okay, I have to admit that I'd had just a few fantasies about him since that first day in his office when he spilled the coffee. And this kiss - well, this kiss exceeded by far my expectations. It is a wonderful, tender, passionate kiss full of longing. The kind of kiss you dream about. Joe couldn't kiss like this.

His lips are so soft and his breath is all minty. When he pulls away from me it leaves me feeling bereft and wanting. His eyes are hooded as he looks down at me.

"Are you seeing anyone?" He asks suddenly.

I'm pulled back to the present by his question. "No," I answer honestly. "Why?"

I've no idea why I asked him that when the answer to the question was so blatantly apparent. He had, after all just kissed me in the elevator.

"Because," he states matter of fact, "I want to fuck you and I need to know what, if anything is standing in my way."

I'm taken aback, to say the least, by his rather bold statement. For a split second I almost get angry, but then recognition sparks in my mind; the elevator scene; the indecent proposal - and it suddenly all becomes so clear.

As a kid growing up my mom used to get so upset with me when I would laugh at my siblings for something silly they had done. As a result I had learned to hide behind a phony mask of sincerity to keep from hurting their feelings.

I was attempting to do this now - and failing miserably at it. The tick started in my left eye then moved down to the corner of my mouth. It was only a matter of time before he thought I was having a full blown seizure. I just couldn't hold it back. I started laughing. Not just a giggle, this was a full blown, bent over double, laugh until you cry with your face in your hands, belly laugh. And I couldn't stop.

Adam looked at me in horror as I laughed so hard I thought I might pee myself. My face must have been beet red. I could barely breathe, I was laughing so hard.

The poor man was stuck in an elevator with a near hysterical woman, who by all rights was probably reacting to the crappy day I'd had up till now, as much as the corny pick-up line.

I felt so bad for him but I just couldn't stop laughing. Finally I got a grip on myself and looked up at him to see him running his hand through his hair. I was heaving deep breaths trying to stifle the laughter that was still bubbling up.

"I'm so sorry," I tried. "Should I call you Gideon?" I said as the laugh resurfaced momentarily.

Adam slumped back against the elevator wall in defeat. "That obvious huh?" he asked.

I smiled. "That was cute."

"Look," he said looking mortified, "I'm really sorry. That was stupid, I know, I just didn't know how to start talking to you." He was running his hands through his hair again.

Reaching up I took him by the wrists and pulled his hands down. Despite the fact that most any other woman would have been, at the very least offended, if not downright angry, I was actually happy. The truth was he had made me laugh, and god knows I really needed it. I couldn't remember the last time I'd felt so good inside. For the last several months I'd spent more time crying than anyone should ever have to cry in a lifetime. I actually felt alive again as I smiled up at him.

"You had me at the kiss Adam."

His eyes lit up at my words. "Really?" He asked in amazement.

"Really," I replied. "Of course now I might need a little reminder."

He didn't have to be told twice. Stepping closer he pulled me against him, his lips claiming mine once again. *Oh god – yes, it's just as good as I remembered.*

We were suddenly jerked, falling against the wall, as the elevator came back to life and finished its descent.

"Let's go get some lunch." He said taking my hand when the door opened. I didn't even resist but allowed him to lead me across the lobby out the front entrance and onto the sidewalk. The sun had made an appearance after all.

Once outside he turned to me. "There's a little bistro about a block down. Is that okay?"

I smiled. "That will be fine. I was actually headed there myself."

We walked the distance in relative silence still holding hands until we reached the establishment. At that point he released my hand and placed his at the small of my back, guiding me toward the seating area. We sat at one of the umbrella tables outside, opposite each other. A waiter came and took our drink orders.

"So," I started, "that was some ice breaker back there. What made you use that one?"

Adam grinned embarrassed. "Well, it was actually my friend's idea – sort of. I asked him for some pointers on talking to a girl. He gave me some books and told me to read them. He seemed to think that was what women wanted to hear."

I laughed but I was so impressed with his honesty. "So you thought you'd use a line from the book?"

"Well, not actually, that's just how it worked out. That's definitely not something I do on a regular basis. "He said smiling again. "So I take it you've read that book?"

"Only four or five times," I said admittedly.

He hung his head in embarrassment. "I just can't believe it. I'd never even heard of it before. Do you know other people who've read it?"

"I don't know anyone personally who hasn't – except some guys. So you've read it?"

"Well, parts of it at least." He was grinning again.

I asked, genuinely curious. "You don't seem to be the type that has trouble picking up a girl." On the contrary I had been shocked to learn that he didn't have a string of women waiting in line for him; he was that good looking.

"You'd be surprised." He stated, and then added for clarification. "Usually I don't have a problem unless it's someone I find extremely attractive. It didn't help that it was almost impossible for me to even talk to you. I've been trying for two weeks now just to say hi. Things just kept coming up that prevented me approaching you. I thought the elevator might be my only chance. There was no one there to cut me off or drag you away to the dance floor."

I smiled, noting his reference to the pub. "You seem to be doing okay talking to me now. Does that mean you don't find me attractive?"

He laughed. "No, I think it means I've already humiliated myself in front of you in the worst possible way and survived. It can only get better from here. I just hope you're not going to start avoiding me again."

I felt a stab of regret. I sighed. "I'm sorry for that honestly. I wasn't really trying to avoid you. It's just..." I paused for a moment trying to collect my thoughts.

"When I first got here I was still struggling with a bad break-up I'd gone through months ago. I had to kind of fake it just to get through the day. It's not that I wasn't attracted to you, I was...am."

He had laid all of his cards out on the table. I felt I should too. It was only fair that I be honest with him. He had been brutally honest with me. "I guess I was hoping all along that my ex would come back into my life and things would go back to how they used to be. It wasn't until today, when he called me in the middle of a very bad morning, that I suddenly realized I didn't want things the way they used to be. What used to be had not been enough for me."

Adam leaned back in his chair. "So you are over him?" It was more of a question than a statement.

"Yes." I stated emphatically. "I'm not saying I don't still hurt some, but I'm finally ready to move on without him. It's very liberating."

Adam leaned forward and squeezed my hand. "I'm not asking for a commitment, just the chance for us to get to know each other. Take a chance with me. If it doesn't work out then at least you've had someone fun to date and maybe I'll learn how to talk to a pretty woman without making a disaster of it. I'd really like the chance to get to know you."

I nodded. "Okay," I agreed. He wasn't asking me to marry him or even to be exclusive. He just wanted us to get to know each other. Surprisingly I found myself wanting that too. "I'll take a chance," I said smiling. "But for future reference you probably shouldn't use that line again."

He shook his head laughing. "I think you're probably right."

We ate our lunch then and headed back to the office.

"Can I have your number?" He asked me on the walk back.

73

I flipped through my contacts and dialed his number. He was surprised when his phone started ringing.

"That's my number." I said. "Just save it in your contacts."

"You already had my number?" He asked with an eyebrow raised.

"I have all the numbers in our directory. It makes it easier when I need to call someone."

"Even Ned's?" He asked frowning. I laughed.

"Yes, even Ned's." Then remembering my plans for a new phone I added. "But that number is going to change ASAP. I'm going after work to get a new phone. I've needed one for a while and after the phone call this morning a new number will be great too."

Adam smiled. "Just as long as you call me with the new one; I'd rather your ex didn't call you either."

Getting back on the elevator to go to my floor I smiled. I would never again think of elevators in the same way. Adam stuffed his hands in his pockets and leaned against the back wall. I knew he was thinking the same thing.

I looked up at him through my lashes. He stood, rocking up onto his toes for a second then blurted out, "Oh to hell with it." And once again we were kissing in the elevator...

Adam stepped out of the elevator and headed straight to his office. He had spent more time at lunch then he had planned to and had a few things he needed to finish up. However, once he got there he was unable to focus on the task at hand. His mind kept returning to his lunch with Drew, and the elevator ride to the lobby.

He laughed at himself, still embarrassed by what he'd said. Drew had referred to it as an ice breaker. It was an ice breaker alright, and a defense breaker and pride buster. He had nothing left to hide behind when it came to Drew. Those few minutes in the elevator had completely exposed him, making him totally vulnerable in her presence.

The odd part was that it also made him completely comfortable with her. She had seen him at one of his worst moments and had not gone running for the hills. This was a real confidence booster. Talking to Drew had been pretty much like talking to any other girl, except that he immensely enjoyed talking to and spending time with her.

Drew's guard seemed to have been down today too and he assumed it had something to do with her ex. For a minute, when she entered the elevator it looked like she might have been crying. Maybe that was why she'd been as open and honest with him as she was. Whatever the reason, he didn't want to give her time to build her wall back. He needed to take every advantage he could.

Picking up his phone he scrolled through his contacts, then sent her a text asking her to have dinner with him.

He looked at the paperwork on his desk. He needed to get it finished up, but right now, seeing Drew again was more important.

When I got off on my floor I was smiling and there was a definite spring to my step. Amy noticed immediately.

"Wow, what a difference a lunch hour can make. You look like you're feeling better hon."

I flashed a face splitting grin at her before taking a seat at my desk. Immediately my computer pinged with a new email.

--- > Ok, spill it chick. I want to know what happened to you at lunch.

I laughed as I typed my reply. Amy would die if she had to wait, now that her curiosity was piqued.

--- > Not on company email, I'll tell you at home.

I had barely fired it off before my computer was pinging again.

--- > You mean you're going to make me wait a whole hour and a half???

--- > Yep!

Ned poked his head around the partition trying to see what was on my screen. I smiled and turned my monitor just out of his view.

"What are you two girls up to?" He asked. "It sounds like computer Ping-Pong in here."

Suddenly Ned's computer pinged and he jumped back to his desk to read his incoming message.

"Oh very funny Amy, mind my own business huh?"

"This is girl talk Ned," Amy said tartly. "Unless you have some input on what kind of tampons we should use."

Ned groaned. "It must be something really juicy or you wouldn't be trying to distract me with feminine hygiene products."

My cell phone started buzzing and I picked it up expecting to see a text from Amy. It was Adam.

Would you do dinner with me tonight???

I quickly texted him back. I already had plans with Amy – sort of – at least for the wine.

Sorry – Plans with Amy tonight.

My phone buzzed again.

She could come too☺. Or I could pick something up??

I thought about it for a minute. It would be fun but I wanted to run it by Amy first. I quickly stepped around the corner into her cubicle. Hands on her desk; I leaned close to her, talking so that Ned couldn't hear.

"How would you feel about dinner with me and a friend tonight?"

Amy leaned back in her chair and folded her arms across her chest. Her face puckered into a frown as she eyed me up and down.

"Joe didn't show up in town did he? Is that what you did at lunch?"

A smile spread across my face lighting my eyes as I slowly shook my head. Amy's eyes got as big as saucers and her mouth formed a big O.

"Ohmygod, ohmygod, ohmygod, ohmygod, ohmygod." She said in rapid succession. "Yes, yes, yes!!" She said clapping her hands together. "Are we going out or staying in?"

"I'm not sure. Does it matter to you?"

Amy shook her head, "Nope."

"Okay, I'll let you know."

I went back to my desk and texted Adam that dinner would be fine. A moment later the phone at my desk rang. He had decided it would be easier to make plans on the phone rather than texting.

We opted to eat in at mine and Amy's place. He would stop and pick-up some Italian food and I would get the wine, after getting my phone.

Ned was huffing in his cubicle when he overheard me making dinner plans. He didn't know who it was with but I could tell he wasn't happy.

SIX

At five o'clock sharp, just as I was clocking out, my phone buzzed again with a text message. I pulled it out of my purse while I waited at the elevators with Amy. It was a message from Joe.

Drew please call me. I really need to talk to you. Please…

I closed my eyes and took a deep breath then stuffed the phone back into my purse.

Amy looked over at me. "Was that Joe again?"

I nodded.

Amy sighed. "The sooner we get your new phone the better." I wholeheartedly agreed.

Amy stopped by my car before heading to hers. I'd forgotten that we'd taken separate vehicles this morning since I was running so late. She drummed her fingernails on the roof as I buckled my seatbelt.

Leaning into the window she smiled. "You are going to spill every last detail of whatever it was that caused you to come back from lunch with that shit-eating grin on your face."

"I will." I promised.

"But right now you have to tell me. Is it Adam that's coming over?"

I nodded smiling. "Yes."

Amy pumped her fist in the air. "Yes!" She spouted. "Good for you."

"Listen, since we're in separate cars, why don't I just stop and get stuff and you can go on home. There's no since in both of us driving around."

"Okay," Amy agreed. "I'll call you if I think of anything else we need while you're out."

I stopped at the cellular store first but the phone I really wanted was out of stock and it was going to take three days before it came in. I decided to order it and wait rather than get something I really didn't want. With that done I stopped by the market and found a couple of nice wines and a tiramisu for desert.

I had just pulled out of the market when my phone rang. Thinking it might be Amy I grabbed it from my purse and answered it without looking to see who it was.

My heart sank in my chest when I heard Joe's voice on the line again.

"Drew please - please don't hang up. I really need to talk to you."

I took a deep breath. I just couldn't frigging believe that he was calling me after all these months, just when I was finally starting to pull out of my funk. I was on the verge of tears again already and decided I should pull over before I caused an accident.

"What is it that you need to tell me now that could possibly be so important you waited eight months to say?" I asked angrily. "I have not heard a single thing from you since the day you left and now you just expect me to want to talk to you?"

"No, I don't expect you to want to talk to me." He said rather humbly. "But I'm begging you Drew, please. I know I fucked up. I knew it right after I left but was too ashamed to come back by then. I knew I'd hurt you. I'm sorry, so very sorry Drew. Please give me another chance."

I exhaled into the phone. "I'm sorry too Joe, but you waited too long to figure this out. I'm moving on now. In fact I'm going this minute to meet someone for dinner."

"Please Drew; I know I hurt you…"

"You're damn right you hurt me." I said, angrily cutting him off, as everything I'd wanted to say before but couldn't now flowed out of my mouth in a steady stream. "Do you realize you didn't even tell me goodbye when you left? Do you know how hard it was for me to see you everywhere I went? Especially seeing how apparently happy you were when I was so fucking miserable."

"Do you have any idea what my life's been like these last months? No you don't. Because you never once stopped to check, not even to have your mother call and ask me how I was. If you had, you would have known that I was devastated. You would have known the reason I moved away was because it was killing me to see you."

"I had to get away so I could reclaim my life. And now that I'm finally starting to move on you pop back into my life and just expect me to drop what I'm doing for you. I probably would have done that just a short time ago, but I won't now. Please don't call me again Joe."

"Okay," he said. "I won't call you again. If you tell me right now that you don't still love me. I will hang up and you will never hear from me again. Just say it."

I couldn't say it. I knew I should, just to make him go away, but I couldn't bring myself to say those five words. The truth was I did still love him. I didn't want to anymore, and I was making an honest effort to get over him but I couldn't bring myself to say the words. Instead I choked on my own tears.

"That's what I thought." He said on the end of the line.

"Goodbye Joe," was all I could manage as I hung up the phone.

I arrived back at the apartment just before six. Amy took one look at me and grabbed the bag of wines from me.

"Holy hell Drew, please tell me he didn't call you again."

I shook my head. "I am so screwed." I cried. "My phone won't be in for another three days. He is not going to leave me alone now because I couldn't tell him I don't love him anymore."

Amy pulled me into a hug and then poured me a glass of wine.

"I don't know what to do now." I said. "Should I just tell Adam not to come?"

"Oh hell no," Amy nearly shouted. "Today was the first time I've really seen you smile since you got here. The only thing Joe has managed to do is make you cry again. It doesn't matter that you still love him. What matters is that your love for him is hurting you."

"It's not healthy anymore. You need to feel alive again like you did today with Adam. He'll be here in an hour. Drink your glass of wine and go shower. Wash all this crap down the drain." Then holding out her hand she raised her eyebrows. "And leave your phone with me."

I did as Amy said, glad that someone could tell me what to do right now. She was normally right about such things. Come to think about it, I probably wouldn't be in this situation now if I'd listened to her when she said not to move in with Joe.

As the hot water ran over my head the wine started kicking in and I began to feel much better. I got out of the shower and dressed, reapplying my makeup.

This would be the second time today that Adam had to see me post cry. Once again I used my eye drops and some cream to help reduce swelling. By the time Adam arrived I would look like normal again.

Walking out into the kitchen Amy handed me my phone back.

"The two numbers you had listed for Joe will go straight to voicemail from now on. Just be sure not to answer if you don't recognize the number. We'll get you through the next couple of days. If he texts you just try to delete them without reading."

"Thanks Amy," I said hugging her again as she poured me another glass of wine.

Adam arrived at seven with the food, and all thoughts of Joe disappeared. He was so good looking and freshly showered. That feeling of giddiness returned and before long he had me laughing again.

We all made plates and carried them into the living room where we watched re-runs of "Big Bang Theory" and ate leaning against the couch using the coffee table for our drinks.

After dinner Amy disappeared to her room. "Just so you know I won't be hanging around all evening after dinner with you guys." She had said giving me a wink. "I've got some serious reading to catch up on in that new book I downloaded. Looks like it's gonna be another scorcher."

Already my phone was flashing at me with notifications of voice mails. When it started buzzing with text messages I turned it off.

Adam noticed. "Your ex?" He asked, one eyebrow raised.

"Yes, unfortunately he decided to make my day living hell."

"So, no new phone then," he asked, genuinely concerned.

"It had to be ordered. I should get it Thursday. Until then Amy fixed it so that his calls would go to voicemail."

Adam turned to face me while still leaning against the couch. His head propped against a fist. His other hand traced the curve of my face with his fingertips.

"You said today that when you came here you were struggling with the breakup. Are you still?"

I nodded. "Yes, a bit." I said honestly.

Little sirens were blasting in my head as Adam leaned closer to me.

"I'd like to make you forget him."

My heart was pounding in my chest when his lips closed over mine. Just like earlier in the elevator, his lips were so soft. His hand was now on the back of my head, holding me in place as his mouth eagerly devoured every inch of mine.

I was so lost in him. Tentatively I explored with my tongue, tasting first the crease of his lips then the tip of his own tongue as he opened his mouth to me.

He pulled me closer; both arms now wrapped around my body as our tongues languidly explored each other, my hands on his back and in his hair.

With physical effort he pulled away, leaving us both with heaving chest and ragged breathing. If his kisses were any indication of what he could do in bed he must be fantastic.

Having only been with Joe I had never slept with someone on a first date but I wanted to now. Technically, I told myself, if I counted lunch today, this was actually our second date.

I smiled to myself for my shamelessness. For the first time in my life I actually wanted to have sex with someone other than Joe. I was really moving on.

Still in the back of my mind I knew that quite possibly I was just trading one heart ache for another. Incredible as it was though; I was more concerned about Adam than I was myself. I didn't want to hurt him in the process of getting over Joe.

Adam grinned at me and kissed me on the forehead. "Sorry I got so carried away. I know I shouldn't be pushing you. You're just so tempting."

I laughed, "Back at you."

Adam pushed a wayward strand of hair behind my ear. "I really do want to get to know you Drew. I want to spend as much time with you as you'll let me."

We spent the next two hours talking about family and friends. I learned that the guy I'd seen him with at the gym was his best friend Davy. He wanted me go with him one day to meet Davy and his girlfriend Gloria.

He had a few other good friends that he spent time with when he could but most of them now had significant others which had changed the dynamics of their relationship. Only one other of his good friends was still single.

Like me, Adam came from a large family. He had two brothers and two sisters. He was the middle child and had grown up in a big house in a rural part of Everett Washington, just north of Seattle. Being close to the water he had spent a lot of time in and on it as a kid.

As was apparent, he was in to fitness and went to the gym at least a couple times a week. I admitted to not making it to the gym as often as I wanted to. He invited me to go with him in the morning before work on Wednesday and I took him up on his offer. It would be nice have someone to workout with again.

We made plans to go out Friday evening. He was going to try to get some of his friends together and I'd get Amy to go along. I was looking forward to meeting Adam's friends.

It was late when he got up to go home and as much as I hated him leaving I knew I would never get up in the morning if he didn't.

Before he left I split the rest of the lasagna and salad up into separate containers for lunch the next day and put some in a bag for him to take.

We said our goodbyes on the front porch and once again I had to resist the urge to drag him back to my bedroom. I stood on the top step and watched until he drove out of the parking lot.

As soon as I walked back inside I was met by Amy.

"OMG girl I thought he'd never leave. I'm dying here. I need details. How did all this happen?"

I plopped down on the couch grinning and told Amy the whole story. Her eyes got round as saucers when I told her about the elevator and I thought she might roll on the floor laughing.

"Well that was definitely not very professional of him." She laughed.

"Oh I don't know about that. If he got any more professional I would have had to pay him for it."

"That's not what I meant and you know it." She said still laughing. "So I was right about him being shy." She said then.

"Yea, but you have to promise me you'll never mention this to anyone. He was embarrassed enough."

Amy held her right hand up with two fingers spread in a V, pointing them at her eyes, her nose between them. "Witch's honor," She said smiling while crossing her heart with her other hand.

I powered my phone back on before getting into bed. Immediately I got a text from Adam.

Night!

I smiled as I texted back.

Goodnight!

SEVEN

Just as Monday had been horribly disastrous, Tuesday proved to be just the opposite. I was awake on time feeling well rested and rode with Amy to work. I quickly finished up the bookwork for Randy's friend and was able to get back on my regular assignment.

At lunchtime Amy and I went up to the rooftop with Adam. After clearing the table and chairs of water from a recent rain, we ate our leftover lasagna and salad.

On the way back down Amy turned around to tell me something and caught Adam and me kissing in the corner. I guess the elevator was just going to be our thing.

Joe continued to call and text me all day long but I ignored it as much as possible. I was glad the calls were going to voicemail and the texts I just deleted as I saw them. Adam was texting me too so it was easy to not even look at the texts from Joe.

I knew I was rebounding and that I should be taking things slower but I honestly didn't know how and didn't want to if I could.

That night as I went to bed my phone buzzed again and I picked it up and read the text from Adam.

Sweet dreams!

I couldn't help but smile as I quickly texted back,

Goodnight – you too!

Then turned out the light and climbed into bed.

Adam lay awake for just a while staring at the text from Drew. He smiled to himself as he read it again. He couldn't believe things were going so well with her.

She was such a beautiful woman and he'd never expected her to actually like him. He was still thinking about the events of the week when he heard someone at the front door.

Getting out of bed he went to see who it was. It was nearly midnight and couldn't imagine who would show up at his place this late.

Looking through the peephole he couldn't believe his eyes. It was Drew. He hurriedly opened the door for her.

She was in his arms in an instant, kissing him hungrily, her hands fisting in his hair. His hands were all over her, pulling her close, feeling the firmness of her body as her mouth moved greedily down his throat to his chest.

He was panting when he pulled away from her.

"If you keep kissing me like this I won't be able to stop myself."

"I don't want you to." She said looking at him with sultry eyes.

She stepped back and pulled her dress over her head. She now stood before him in nothing but a pair of black stiletto sandals. Adam ran his hands through his hair. He had dreamed of this and she was just as gorgeous as he'd imagined, all the way down to her Brazilian wax.

His cock was so hard it was straining against his pajama pants as he picked her up and carried her to his bed. Laying her down in the bed he stood back and looked at her as he slowly removed his pants allowing his erection to spring free.

Where to start? There were so many things he wanted to do to this woman that he'd never done before. He'd never wanted to do them to anyone else, but Drew was different.

Now looking down at her with her bare pussy he knew he wanted to put his tongue right between the folds. He wanted to lap into the entrance of her body until she came on his face and then sink his cock deep inside while she screamed out his name.

She was writhing on the bed beneath his stare, her body arching up. Her head moving side to side as she fisted the sheets. He wanted her now. He couldn't hold back.

Climbing between her legs he lowered himself slowly into her, feeling her warmth, listening to her moans. She felt so good. Too damn good. He wanted this to go on forever as he started moving inside her......

Adam jerked suddenly awake, his heart beating out of his chest. Sweat was beaded on his forehead and he realized he was grasping his cock. His thigh was covered with the stickiness from his wet dream. *Shit!*

Getting out of bed he stripped the sheets off. His phone was stuffed under his pillow. He must have fallen asleep looking at it. Carrying the sheets to the utility room, he put them in the washing machine and turned it on. He couldn't believe it. He hadn't had a wet dream since he was a teenager, but damn it was good. He wouldn't mind having one about Drew every night.

Grabbing a clean set of sheets he took them to his room, his thoughts going to Drew. Damn he wanted her. He'd do just about anything to keep her in his life. He hoped she wanted him too.

EIGHT

I was on the treadmill when Adam came into the gym. He told me he gave himself forty-five minutes for his workout and I had wanted at least thirty to run so I came a few minutes early.

He disappeared into the locker room then a minute later was standing next to me.

"Morning," he said looking at the readout on my treadmill. I'd already been on twenty-five minutes. "So you're a runner huh?"

"Yes, I started running in school, you?"

"No, I just warm up. I was never too good at running distance."

"That's okay. I'll be done by the time you finish your warm up and we can hit the weights together."

Ten minutes later we were heading downstairs for the weight machines. Adam stopped me and pointed to a small cove.

"Wanna take the elevator?" He grinned.

I laughed. "It's only one floor."

"So, I bet there's an emergency stop button in there."

He grabbed my hand as we trotted down the stairs.

"You sure are frisky this morning." I said eyeing him suspiciously.

"I had a good night last night." He winked.

We finished our workout and went to shower and dress for work. My plan was to pick-up Amy on the way to work if it didn't take too long for me to get ready. I wasn't sure about the shower situation so I told her I'd call if I was running late.

We both had appointments after work for pedicures and I wanted to get my bikini wax. There was no reason to take separate cars unless we just had to.

I showered and dressed in record time and when I left the dressing room I was surprised to see Adam waiting for me.

"I just thought I'd wait around for a minute and walk you to your car if I saw you."

"Thanks, but you didn't have to wait for me."

"I know." He replied taking my gym bag, hoisting it onto his other shoulder. "But I wanted to."

My bag was not light and carrying it in stilettos was much more difficult that it had been in my tennis. I was grateful for the help with the bag, but I knew now I needed to remove some of the unnecessary items.

I opened the trunk for him when we reached my car and he placed the bag inside.

"See you at work." He said getting into his own car.

I waved as I got into mine. Then I left to pick-up Amy.

By eight o'clock my phone was flashing at me, telling me I had voice mail again. By nine there were twenty text messages from Joe, so I was very relieved when the cell store called to say my new phone was available for pick-up. I decided to get it on my lunch hour.

I left a few minutes early to get to the phone store where they transferred my contacts over and had me on my way in fifteen minutes. I was glad I would have enough time to eat the sandwich I brought for lunch.

Entering the lobby I stood waiting at the bank of elevators with a young woman that I figured to be about my age. She was very pretty with long blond hair and deep blue eyes.

As we waited for the car to arrive she glanced down at my feet.

"I love your shoes." She said appreciatively.

"Thank You." I told her.

The elevator arrived and we go in together. I pushed for the fifth floor and asked her which floor.

"Oh," she said looking embarrassed. "I think it's the sixth floor. I don't remember."

"Which department are you looking for?"

Again she looked embarrassed. "I'm not sure about that either. I'm here to see Adam Knight. Would you happen to know where he is?"

My heart suddenly began to sink in my chest. Who was this girl? Why was she here to see Adam?

I nodded trying to find my voice. "Yes, I can show you to his office." I said pushing for the sixth floor.

"Oh thank you so much. He's not expecting me. I just thought I'd show up and surprise him."

I was suddenly incredibly jealous. I knew there really was no cause for it. She hadn't said she was Adam's lover or girlfriend but I was suddenly extremely possessive of him. Still I tried to maintain a nice smile for the rest of the ride in the elevator.

Finally the elevator reached the sixth floor and we exited, the girl following me. My heart was pounding faster with each step towards Adams office. Fear was building inside of me for what I was about to find out. I couldn't believe that it mattered so much to me after only a few days.

We rounded the corner and stepped into Adam's office. He was turned around in his chair facing the computer. I knocked on the door frame.

"Adam." I announced.

He swung around at his desk when he heard my voice, but his eyes landed on the girl next to me. A smile lit his face and he was out of his chair instantly as she squealed and ran into his open arms.

I was suddenly ill. I turned to leave but Adam called my name. I didn't want to witness any more of this. I just needed to get away before I started crying again. But his hand was now on my arm turning me around to face him.

He was still all smiles and I tried to smile myself, but I'm not sure how believable it was. The young woman still had her arms wrapped around his waist.

"Drew," he said. "I want you to meet Lucy, my baby sister."

Shock and relief washed over me instantly and I think my heart skipped a beat. *His sister, oh thank god!* I thought. With them standing together, I realized how much they resembled each other. They had the same blue eyes.

Lucy extended her hand to me and I took it, as a look of realization washed over her face.

"Oh my god," She said looking at Adam. "Is this the Drew you wrote to me about?"

Adam nodded.

So he's already mentioned me to his family!

"Oh my god," she squealed again. "I'm so glad I got to meet you." She said pulling me into a hug. Her joy was infectious and I returned her hug with a huge smile.

As it turned out, Lucy was attending medical school and had a couple weeks off between semesters. She had flown in to visit her parents, and then drove down to see Adam for a few days before returning to school.

She was staying at one of the local hotels with some friends that came into town with her. Adam tried to talk her into staying with him but she declined saying she would visit him but wanted to stay with her friends.

She did however; agree to meet us Friday night saying she would bring her friends out too. I left her and Adam to catch up and ate half of my sandwich before returning to my desk.

Once there I remembered my new phone so I took a few minutes to send my new number to Adam and a few others.

That afternoon Amy and I went for our appointments. I wanted to get my bikini wax done first so that I could relax afterward while I got my pedicure.

My technician was an Asian girl named Tammy and I'd been to her a couple of times since I'd come to Seattle. She was a very pleasant girl and I liked her because she just made conversation while she worked.

As soon as I came into the room she started chatting.

"Howoh honey, how ahw you today?" She said with her pronounced accent.

"I'm good Tammy how are you?"

"Oh honey, you seem so happy today. Why you look so diffewent? You have boyfwien?"

I smiled. "Well, sort of."

"Oh honey, I can tell. You all smile today. What you want to do today?"

"Just the usual bikini wax."

"Oh honey no, bikini wac no good for boyfwien. We do Bwazil for you today. Make you all smooth. Boyfwien like. You see."

108

"Uh, I'm not sure. What is Brazil?"

"Honey we take it all. We make you nice an smooth. You like. You see."

"Won't that hurt?" I asked not sure I wanted this done.

"Only little," Tammy said holding up her thumb and forefinger to show me a small amount. "We do good for you. No much hurt."

"Okay." I said. "I'll try it once."

"Good, good. You like you see. You boyfwein like it nice an smooth."

I removed my skirt and panties and was about to get on the table when my phone rang. Grabbing it from my purse I hopped up and positioned myself on the table then answered it. It was Adam.

"Hey I got your number and wanted to make sure I put it in right. What are you doing?"

I smiled. Tammy was powdering me and putting on the first strip of wax. "Amy and I are getting our toenails done."

That wasn't what I was doing right this moment, but it was the truth.

Tammy jerked the first strip. I was used to this. It wasn't that bad.

"Well, I wanted to ask you. Lucy is coming to my place for dinner tomorrow night. I was hoping you'd come over too."

Tammy jerked the second strip and began applying wax further in. I wasn't sure about going to dinner tomorrow night and Friday. There was stuff I needed to do at home but it was with his sister and she was only in town for a short time.

"Oh...sure, I think that will be fine." I said. "What should I bring?"

"That depends. Do you like Chinese?"

Tammy jerked the next strip as I was answering.

"I love...Holy mother of god!! I said, sucking in air."

"What? Are you alright?"

"Oh sorry," I said with my eyes clenched shut. "Ingrown toenail...she's digging it out. But I love Chinese."

"That sounds brutal... Maybe some wine that goes with Chinese?"

"Yea it is." I said in a high pitch voice as she jerked the next strip. "I could bring some Saki and maybe some Chinese beer." I needed to get off the phone with him - Now.

"That sounds great."

Just then Tammy started talking. "Okay honey, I nee you pull your leg over head."

"What did she just say?" Adam asked.

"Oh, nothing, she just needs a better angle for this toenail. Look can I call you back?"

"Sure. I'll talk to you later."

I hung up as Tammy jerked the last two strips. Note to self: Don't talk on phone while getting waxed.

I stood in front of the full length mirror looking at myself with Amy looking over my shoulder holding her glass of wine.

"Oh my god, I can't believe you let her talk you into that." She said laughing.

I shook my head. "Well one thing's for sure, she was right. It is smooth."

NINE

Thursday after work I came back to the apartment to shower and change. I picked out a pair of jeans and a pullover top. The temperature outside was still relatively mild, below eighty degrees, although I'd heard a few of the locals complaining about the heat. I laughed at the thought. They should spend an August in Austin if they think this is hot.

Looking around in the closet I found my strappy sandals and pulled them on then went to finish dressing in the bathroom. After putting on my makeup I still had some time before I needed to leave so I went to work condensing my gym bag.

I had way too much stuff in the bag making it too heavy to tote back and forth to the gym. I took out all of the unnecessary items then made a list of the stuff I really needed to have but could get in a smaller size. Once done I set it on my bed.

I would be going to the gym in the morning before work so I wanted to put it in my car now. It would be one less thing to worry about in the morning.

Amy had already settled into her recliner with a bottle of cherry coke and a sandwich. Her Kindle was perched in front of her and she was completely engrossed in the story she was reading.

I came and stood in front of her, waiting to see how long it took her realize I was there. After she turned two pages I decided she might never look up.

"I'm leaving now." I said, causing her to jerk her head up. "Must be a good story, I've been standing here two minutes."

She smiled and nodded. "It's an awesome story! You should read this one. The hero is an espionage agent and is totally hot!"

"Okay, have fun reading. I'll see you later."

"I will. You too and if you decide not to come home send me a text and let me know."

"Ha! Yea – alright, if something comes up I'll tell you." I said as I walked out the door. I was pretty sure I'd be back before she went to bed.

I stopped on the way to Adam's and picked up a bottle of Saki and some Tsingtao beer then programmed Adams address into my phone navigator. Ten minutes later I was pulling up at his apartment building.

His apartment was on the second floor so I climbed the steps and knocked. A moment later he opened the door for me. He was wearing nothing but a pair of jeans and his hair was still wet from his recent shower.

"Sorry," he said inviting me in. "I'm running a little late. You can put the beer in the kitchen." He said pointing. "I'll be right back."

I watched him as he walked back into his room. Barefoot and bare backed with tousled curls; he was a site to behold. I stared after him until he disappeared around the corner then went to work putting the beer in the fridge. I'd only had Saki once before and it had been served warm so I left it out on the counter.

His living area was cozy and I occupied my time looking around at his pictures and décor. I saw a picture that I assumed was a group shot of him and his brothers and sisters.

I recognized Lucy right away. She was the youngest, now twenty-four. I didn't know the names of the others but they were all attractive. Only Adam and Lucy had the blue eyes though.

Adam returned to the living room a few moments later. Pulling me into a hug, he kissed me. He smelled of body wash and mint and I leaned into him, feeling the hardness of his chest and arms.

"You look good." He said pulling back to take me in. "I'm glad you could come tonight."

"Me too," I said and really meant it.

"Lucy called a bit ago. She should be here soon. Would you like something to drink? I have some white wine chilled."

"Sure, I'll have a glass of that."

He took down two wine goblets and poured us each one.

"You have a nice place here." I said looking around.

"Here, I'll give you a tour." He said taking me by the hand.

We walked down the hall and he announced each room as if he were a commentator for lifestyles of the rich and famous, speaking with a British accent that was quite impressive.

"On your right you'll notice the fuhst doorway leads into the guest bahth where you can powder your nose or use the toilet in appreciable privacy. The room boasts a porcelain covered, steel bahth-tub complete with a vinyl shower cuhtain."

"Continuing down the grand hall we find the utility room where you can wash, iron, fold, etcetera. You'll notice that by taking the fuhst lettah of each word you can make the acronym W.I.F.E."

I rolled my eyes at him although it was quite funny.

"And now on our left is the Mahstah bedroom suite; exquisitely furnished with solid pine, stained to look like something exotic and rich. Bed coverings imported from France and sold exclusively in the finest French stores – Targét.

You'll notice the mahstah bath has both his and huhr vanities and a showah large enough for two, as long as you have enough soap so that you can slide pahst each othuh."

"Maybe you should take a job as a TV commentator." I said laughing at his comment about the soap.

"Maybe he should just grow up," said a voice from behind us.

Startled we both turned to see Lucy. She was grinning at us as she came to hug Adam.

"Still practicing your British accent I see." Then turning to me, "You know he's been doing that since he was nine. You should hear what other voices he does."

Adam quickly grabbed her up, flinging her over his shoulder as he swatted her on the butt. "And you've been tattling on me since you were three."

He carried her down the hall like that, with her slapping his backside the whole way, giggling as she bounced along. Once in the living room he put her down and kissed her on the forehead.

"You shouldn't be such a brute." She said. "You'll scare all the good girls off."

"I'll take that under advisement." He said smiling. "By the way I'm glad you decided to show up 'cause I'm starving here."

Lucy laughed. "Will you please behave before you frighten my friend off?"

Adam swung around. "What friend?"

On cue a young man stepped from across the room and extended his hand to Adam. "Hi," he said, "I'm Jared."

Adam stood staring at him like a mule looking at a new gate. I quickly stepped up and shook Jared's hand that he still held out, although somewhat awkwardly. Introducing myself, I offered the couple something to drink. Lucy looked relieved. Reluctantly, Adam finally offered his hand, but he continued to watch Jared suspiciously.

I went into the kitchen for a couple of beers. Adam came in behind me sulking. I gigged him in the ribs with a finger.

"Be nice." I said. "He's Lucy's friend and if you trust her then you should also trust her judgment in choosing friends."

Adam sighed. "I know. It's just hard for me to let her grow up. I'm sure this is why she wouldn't stay with me. I'd have made them sleep in separate beds."

I opened the beers and handed them to Adam. "Here, go give him a peace offering and show your sister you can be reasonable." He smiled and bent down, kissing my nose.

"Thanks," he said.

Dinner went well and before long Adam and Jared were talking like old friends. Jared was also in med school. His goal was to be an orthopedic surgeon. Lucy was interested in pediatrics.

By the time the two left Adam had transitioned from being the overprotective brother of his kid sister, to a supportive older brother. Lucy seemed relieved. She was very close to Adam and whether or not he accepted Jared meant a lot to her.

After telling Lucy and Jared goodbye, I began to gather my stuff to leave as well. Adam stopped me, taking my purse off my shoulder and putting it back on the counter.

"Don't leave now." He said rubbing my shoulders. "Stay for a while. It's still early." Lowering his lips to mine he began nibbling, tasting.

Being close to him like this was intoxicating to my senses. He smelled so good and when he pulled me against him I melted into the firmness of his chest. I responded to the passion of his kiss, returning it with the hunger in my own.

My lips parted to allow his tongue entrance; my own tasting and exploring his. His eyes were hooded when he pulled away.

"I've needed this. I haven't had an elevator ride in days now." He said wickedly.

I was near breathless. "I love the way you kiss me, but if you keep it up I won't be able to stop this time."

"I don't want you to stop." He said looking into my eyes. "I want to make love to you Drew. Stay the night with me - please."

There was no way I could tell him no right now. In my mind I envisioned Adam on top of me, covering me, and I wanted him desperately.

"Yes," I whispered. "Let me tell Amy not to expect me home." He nodded.

I grabbed my phone and quickly sent a text that said only "staying" then powered my phone off.

Adam pulled me back into his powerful arms, lifting my chin to meet his kiss. His fingertips gently stroked down my neck to my shoulder as his mouth devoured mine. I was lost in the divine taste and texture that was Adam as our tongues collided and swirled together between parted lips.

Desire burned in my mouth and spread deep in to my groin and my body responded with dampness that moistened my tender folds. With each breath I took I was inhaling Adam. I desired to consume and be consumed by him.

My hands fisted in his hair as his moved to release mine from the tie that held it in place. Then moving them to my back and waist he pulled me firmly against his erection.

I moaned into his mouth in response to the arousal that now possessed me as I attempted to press myself tighter against him. In one swift movement he lifted me into his arms and I wrapped my legs around his waist as he carried me down the hall into his bedroom.

Placing me on his bed he stood back and stripped his shirt off, revealing the perfection of his chiseled chest and arms. A smattering of hair graced his breast bone growing out onto his pecs and formed a line down through his navel and below.

I watched as he unbuckled his belt then stepped forward kneeling before me, pushing between my legs. Gently, while looking into my eyes, he lifted my shirt off over my head. His breath hitched in his throat as he took in the swell of my breast behind the lace of my bra.

"You are so perfect." He whispered almost reverently as his fingertips traced the lace along the top of my bra up to the straps. With the same reverence he planted a kiss in the cleft between my breasts before removing my bra.

I had never been with anyone except Joe and had worried that I might be embarrassed to be naked in front of Adam, but I was not. His obvious admiration for my body banished any reservations I may have had.

Rising up, he brought me with him and once again pressed our bodies together, his arms around my back and in my hair as he kissed me. My breasts were pushing into his chest and the friction caused my nipples to bead up tightly.

He stepped back away from me again. "I want to see you." He said; his voice barely a whisper. "I want to see all of you."

Without hesitation I unfastened my pants and pushed them down over my hips. Then stepping out of my sandals, I removed my pants the rest of the way. His eyes were dark and hooded as I slowly and deliberately removed the pair of thong underwear I was wearing.

His eyes wandered slowly down my body and he gasped when they reached my bare sex. He stepped toward me again but I stopped him.

"I want to see you too." I said. My voice filled with longing.

He nodded. Unfastening his pants he pushed them down along with his boxers, freeing his erection. His length was impressive and hung heavily, weighted by the surge of blood through the massive veins there.

Stepping completely out of his pants he once again moved toward me, pushing himself against me. His leg slid between mine and pushed against the apex of my thighs, the moisture of my arousal slick against him.

"I want you Drew, in ways I've never wanted to be with anyone else, I want to be with you." His hand moved down my stomach and beyond until his fingers reached my wet folds. A look of ecstasy was on his face as he pushed a finger into the opening of my core. A surge of pleasure resounded throughout my body.

I reached for his erection. Taking it into my hand I began to stroke the entire length. I felt as it pulsed and grew larger with each touch. Adam screwed his eyes shut for a moment, then lifted me once again, laying me back on the bed.

My legs moved open, inviting him within. I wanted him, ached to feel his cock inside me. He moved between my legs then lowered his mouth to me, licking and tasting, lapping at the entrance to my body, sucking my clit.

My body arched off the bed as waves of pleasure moved through me. My hands fisted in the sheets tightening, mimicking the muscles deep within. Then Adam moved.

"Babe," he said through gritted teeth. "I need to be inside you. I can't wait any longer."

"Yes - please." I begged.

My eyes locked onto his as if searching the depths of his soul. Pools of gorgeous blue opened up to me like windows so I might see past the façade into the inner man. I saw only beauty.

I felt him as he placed his crown at my entrance then slowly pushed inside, watching me as he filled and stretched me to my limit and beyond. He paused for a moment while my body adjusted to his size.

"Are you okay?" he asked.

I nodded. "Yes, but I've got to move." He kissed me then.

"Me too babe," he said. Then slowly he pulled out, almost completely before he pushed back in. My hips pushed up to meet his as we found our rhythm, Adam riding me, pushing me toward climax with each stroke of his beautiful cock. Never before had I experienced sex like this.

We settled into a leisurely pace broken only by the occasional dip of his mouth to my breasts. Lifting his face with my hands I traced the curve of his lips with my thumb, committing it to memory.

Then he shifted, lifting my hips changing the friction points inside me. He began moving faster now and I cried out loudly as he plunged in again and again, sending pulses of pleasure out from my core. The intensity was building stronger. I was on the brink.

"Come for me baby," he growled. "Come with me."

I cried out his name as the pleasure exploded in my core, sending shockwaves throughout my body. Then Adam was moaning through clenched teeth as he found his release, exploding and pulsing deep inside me.

I was lost, so lost in him, already so wrapped up in this man Adam that I didn't know if I'd ever find my way out again.

We collapsed in a tangle of arms and legs, his face nestled into the crook of my neck. After a moment he shifted onto his elbows and gently rocked his pelvis against me. He was still semi hard.

He smiled. "I like being inside of you. I wish I could stay there all night."

I returned his smile, pulling his head down to mine. "I think maybe we could arrange that."

He shifted onto his side, rolling me with him without breaking contact. We were now facing each other and he rose up onto his elbow. Our legs were still entwined and with his free hand he traced the curve of my body.

His expression became serious as he continued to gaze at my body.

"You are so beautiful. Do you know that?"

I smiled shyly at his remark. I didn't think I'd ever been called beautiful before.

He continued. "I must have imagined this moment a hundred times over since the day I met you in my office. It was even better than I imagined." He trailed his fingers down my belly to my sex. "And this," he grinned, "this blew my mind."

I had to laugh at that one. "I have a confession to make." I said trying to be serious. "I wasn't quite honest with you yesterday."

He looked at me with trepidation. I continued.

"Yesterday when I was at the salon talking to you on the phone. She wasn't doing my toenails when I was yelping. She was waxing me. I had hoped you'd like it."

His eyes twinkled with glee and possibly relief. "Like it, I friggin love it." He leaned in and kissed my nose. "I'm sorry that it hurt though. But tonight when I saw that….I thought I might really have a heart attack."

I laughed again. "Well keeping in the spirit of Gideon and all…"

He pursed his lips together and narrowed his eyes at me. Then suddenly without warning pulled out and sat on top of me and started tickling my ribs. I was laughing and squirming beneath him as he continued the sensual torture.

"Beg for mercy wench." He said using his British accent again.

I was laughing too hard to speak now as his fingers poked into the hypersensitive area along my ribcage.

"Please, please." I begged.

"Please what? Tickle you harder?" He said; his face alight with mirth. "Tickle you faster?"

"No, no. Please stop." I begged.

"Please stop what?" He asked with an eyebrow raised.

I couldn't help myself. "Please stop….Gideon."

His eyes got big as saucers as he began tickling harder. "The wench is a cheeky one, is she? Likes the tickle torture, does she?"

"No, no please stop – Adam." I was laughing so hard tears were running back into my hair. Adam stopped then folded over on top of me, pressing himself into me as his mouth claimed me again.

Pulling away he got off of me, extending his hand for me to take. "Let's go wash off."

I followed him into the bathroom where he turned on the water full force in the shower. While we waited for the water to heat Adam dug through his drawers for a T-shirt and a pair of boxer shorts for me to sleep in.

I quickly went to get my purse and dug around in it for a hair tie, then looped my hair through it to keep it out of the water.

My skin was chilled, covered with goose bumps and I stood beneath the hot water of the shower, letting its heat thaw me. Adam stepped in behind me and pulled me against his chest. His mouth went to my neck as his arms snaked around my shoulders.

"I'll drive you home in the morning. What time do you need to be there?" He asked.

"You don't need to do that." I stated. "I can just drive my car. There's no reason for you to get up early for that."

He sighed and turned me around to face him. There was a frown on his face as he gently splashed water onto my shoulders, rubbing at some unseen mark.

"I want to do this Drew. When I asked you to stay with me tonight it wasn't for a convenience fuck. That's not what you are to me."

"I don't think that Adam. I wanted to stay as much as you wanted me too, maybe more."

"Still I don't like the idea of you getting up and driving yourself home. If anyone is going to do that it should be me. Let me take you home this one time. And next time, if you stay here you can bring clothes etc. and get dressed here."

"Alright," I conceded.

It seemed like a lot of effort to shuttle me around when I could just drive my car back and be done with it. As it was he would have to bring me back here later to pick up my car again. Part of me was glad though. I remembered numerous times when this scene had played out with Joe. I went to his place, had sex then he'd sent me home. Now, thinking back on it I realized I'd been just what Adam had said, a convenience fuck. I'd been used.

No wonder it had been so easy for Joe to walk away. I was just a convenience for him. Adam was different. He thought differently of me.

Wrapping my arms around his waist I lay my head against his chest. "Thank you." I said.

I woke the next morning to gentle kisses on my neck and shoulders. "Wake up sleepyhead." Adam said in my ear. I brushed my hair out of my face.

"What time is it?" I asked.

"Five-thirty, you never told me when you needed to be home."

"Ugg," I groaned squeezing my eyes shut again.

"You know you snore something dreadful." Adam said.

"What?" I said sitting up in the bed. "Uh-uh! Really?" I was awake now.

"No, I'm just messing with you. But you're awake now. We need to get you home so you can get ready."

I cut my eyes at him. Then suddenly I remembered something. "Hey, isn't this denim Friday?"

Adam thought a minute. "Yes I think so."

"Then I can just wear the clothes I came over here in."

"Do you have everything else you need?"

"My gym bag is in the trunk of my car. My makeup bag and everything is in it. I think even a clean pair of panties."

Adam wagged his eyebrows at me. "Maybe we have time for a quickie then."

I grinned. "We may have time for a full workout!"

Adam jumped up. "Here, give me your keys and I'll run get your bag."

Getting up I went to the bathroom where I'd left my purse the night before. Handing him my keys I turned to use some of his mouthwash and finger comb my hair.

Adam was back in a flash, depositing my bag on the bathroom floor then used some of the mouthwash himself. Turning he gave me a wicked grin then scooped me up and over his shoulder, carrying me into the bedroom once again.

"Didn't Lucy just tell you not to do stuff like this?" I asked as he dropped me on the bed.

"Yes, and I took it under advisement." He said still grinning.

His impossible blue eyes sparkled with humor as his smile exaggerated the dimple in his cheek. He wasted no time divesting me of the T-shirt and boxers he'd loaned me. Then kneeling up on his knees he looked down at me like an artist admiring his handiwork.

He sat for a moment, his lower lip caught between his teeth, before rising up and opening the blinds. The first rays of dawn were spreading across the sky now. Dim light filtered into the room.

"I want to see you in the light." He said climbing back onto the bed. His hand went immediately to my bare sex as his fingers skimmed the exposed, baby soft skin.

With each gentle touch my arousal was growing stronger. His eyes closed as he slipped a finger inside of me and started moving it around. I lifted my hips in response, pushing against the palm of his hand.

When he opened his eyes again they were dark and dilated. "Baby, you are so wet already. I can feel that tight little pussy squeezing and pulling on my finger."

Already my breathing was ragged. Desire spread throughout my being. I craved his touch. I was left feeling bereft as he withdrew his finger to remove his pajama pants. His erection springing free evoked a primal response in me. I wanted to taste him.

I licked my lips, my mouth suddenly dry. "I want you in my mouth." I whispered hoarsely.

His eyes widened but he moved closer on the bed to me. His cock was pulsing as a surge of blood filled the massive vein, eliciting a drop of pre-cum which I licked off eagerly.

I liked the way he tasted, the texture of his velvet skin stretched over stone. I took his plush crown into my mouth feeling him shudder as I swirled my tongue around it.

I released him, pushing him back onto the bed. It was my turn to pleasure him. I wanted to see and feel him come unglued beneath my touch.

I took him once again into my mouth, working the base of his impressive cock with my hands while sucking and swirling the head with my tongue.

He began to pump his hips against me as I bobbed my head up and down along his length, taking him almost entirely into my mouth. He looked down at me and I caught his gaze as I continued to work his length. The look of pleasure drove me to give him more. He was close, I could tell by the way he swelled even larger in my mouth, and I moved faster and sucked harder pushing him over the edge.

His head fell back into the bed and his eyes screwed shut, a moan escaping from deep in his throat as his cock began to pulse out his cum. I swallowed, keeping him far back in my throat and continued to suck.

He was still moaning as his body convulsed from the intensity of his incredible orgasm. Finally, as his tremors subsided, I moved up alongside him in the bed.

"That was amazing." He said almost breathless.

I smiled and kissed him. It truly was amazing. I had never done that before; had never wanted to before. But I wanted to with Adam.

I had everything I needed for work but I still called Amy and asked her to bring my stiletto pumps and a button down top. She did and I changed in the restroom at work.

I smiled to myself as I thought about the kiss in the elevator today. He was getting bolder every day and I cautioned him to not get in trouble at work. He just winked at me and kissed me again as the elevator glided to a stop on my floor.

TEN

Adam sat at his desk looking over a stack of reports when his phone rang. He looked at the number halfway hoping it to be Drew, but it was not. The number was from the upstairs offices. One he recognized as belonging to Larry Jameson, the owner and CEO of the company.

He couldn't figure out why he'd be calling but he hoped it wasn't because someone had complained about him kissing in the elevators. He smiled to himself. No one had seen him – yet.

He answered the phone.

"Adam Knight."

"Hello Adam, this is Larry. How have you been?"

"Good, sir, and yourself?"

"Oh as well as can be expected I guess. Arthritis has been giving me fits in my knee again.

Doctor says the erosion has gotten worse and I'm going to need a knee replacement soon."

"Sorry to hear that sir. What can I do for you?"

"Well Adam, I've wanted to talk to you about something and was hoping you could come up to the office around three. I'll be in meetings all day until then."

"Yes sir, I can be there. Is there anything I need to bring? Reports, etc.?"

"No not today. Just a friendly chat, that's all."

"Very good, sir, I'll see you then."

"Okay Knight. See you at three."

Adam hung up the phone. This was unusual for Larry to call him. He had always liked the man and had never had a problem in the eight years he'd worked for him. He felt that Larry had liked him as well and had always been a fair employer. Larry was sharp as a tack when it came to business but he was highly family-oriented and never allowed his business to run him. This was yet another reason that Adam respected the man.

At ten to three Adam made his way to the elevators. He was a bit anxious about this meeting;

Drew's warning making him just the slightest bit paranoid now. Stepping off the elevator onto the eighth floor he stopped in front of the reception desk outside Larry's office.

Margaret, the receptionist looked up and smiled at Adam. She was an older woman in her fifties that took care of most secretarial things for Larry.

"Good afternoon Mr. Knight, Mr. Jameson has been expecting you. You can go on in."

Adam walked around the desk and pushed through the massive oak door. Mr. Jameson's office was large but homey with overstuffed furniture and pictures of family everywhere.

The older man was sitting behind a massive mahogany desk. He looked up and smiled when Adam walked in. Despite the smile he was looking older than the last time Adam had met with him. Weariness showed in his gray eyes.

Behind him to the right was a shelf filled with pictures of Brianna, Larry's granddaughter. Adam had met her once before at a company picnic. She was about Drew's age if he remembered correctly and also had long brown hair.

He thought about the last time they'd spoken; Larry had mentioned her being in Europe studying.

"Come in and have a seat my man." Larry said, motioning to one of the chairs.

Adam nodded and took a seat.

"I guess you're wondering why I've called you up here," Larry said eyeing him.

Adam nodded. "Yes sir, the thought has crossed my mind."

"Well put you mind at ease. I just wanted to run something by you."

Adam visibly relaxed then.

"I am looking into expanding the company, nothing major but a small branch or two. As you know, I need a knee replacement and can no longer get around like I used to. And even if I could I no longer have the desire to be out here in the work-a-day world.

I'm ready to retire and play golf for a while. Maybe go to Europe and see Brianna. I think she may not be coming back. It seems some young Brit has stolen her heart.

Anyway when I was kicking this idea around in my head I thought of you. You do good work and are young and still have lots of energy. I wanted to run this by you and see what you thought.

I haven't made any final decisions yet but I was wondering if you might want to step up into more of a director position for this startup company. You would have several managers beneath you. Of course a few above you that you'd have to answer to but I feel that you could do the job well."

Adam was taken aback. Growing with the company had always been his goal but this was a great offer.

He swallowed the lump in his throat. "It sounds like a great opportunity. Would it require me to relocate?"

"Relocating wouldn't be necessary, not unless you wanted to. It would be a bit of a commute though. The position I have in mind for you would be across the ferry. I'm looking to open it on Bainbridge Island. So many of our customers now have to ride the ferry to get here. It would make it more convenient for them and of course we could reach others if we were there."

"How soon are you looking for this to happen?"

"Within the next six to nine months. Things haven't started moving yet but when they do it will be fast. So are you interested?"

"Yes - absolutely."

"Great, great, well keep it under your hat for the time being and I'll get back with you on it later."

Adam left Larry's office then. This was more than he'd expected and it was a great opportunity. Larry had said to keep it under his hat, but he would still run it by Drew. He smiled at the thought. He liked having her around; liked being able to talk about things like this.

The day passed in a blur and soon it was time to go. I glanced at my phone. The absence of phone calls and texts from Joe was a mental boost. I loved my new phone if only for that reason.

Waiting at the elevators with Amy, Adam emerged from the stairwell and came to join us. He was all smiles as we packed into the crowded elevator for the ride to the lobby.

It was five o'clock on a Friday afternoon. Everyone who hadn't left early for the day was now cramming into the elevator to leave.

Adam pulled me snugly against his side and planted a kiss on the side of my face.

Ned, who had thought he'd seen something turned to glare at Adam. Adam met his gaze and pulled me closer against him, if that were possible, then kissed me again to make sure Ned saw. Ned turned away in a huff.

"Be nice." I whispered to Adam.

"I am being nice. You didn't see me give him the bird did you?" I gigged him in the ribs.

Leaving the building he walked with Amy and me to our cars.

"We'll see you at eight." I said.

"Alright," he said as I got into the car, then leaning into the window, "I have some news to share – when we have a few minutes alone again."

"Okay," I said, wondering what his news was.

We met at the same bar we'd met at before with the group from the office. Since the weather was so warm Amy and I opted to wear dresses.

My dress was black and sleeveless with a yoke collar that was embellished with metallic looking stones. It was an airy dress with a flutter skirt and a gathered waist. The skirt stopped about four inches above my knee and I wore some strappy black stiletto sandals with it.

Amy was also wearing black but hers was a tight fitting stretch dress with cutouts down both sides. It was incredibly sexy and she was incredibly hot with all her curves. Her shoes were black platform sandals and she topped the look with a black fedora. All eyes turned to her as we entered the building. I smiled to myself. *Just wait till you see her dance guys!*

Lucy and a group of her friends were already waiting at a table and they motioned us over. One of her guy friends, who I later learned was Paul, was completely smitten with Amy. His eyes followed her everywhere she went.

Adam showed up just a few minutes after we did looking all yummy. I honestly thought he would look good if he'd dressed himself in a paper bag. I watched as a couple of girls at the bar turned to ogle as he walked by; their hopes dashed to pieces when he walked up and kissed me. I was on top of the world.

I sat and talked with Lucy getting to know her and her friends over a chocolate martini. Amy had a row of drinks lined up for her, sent from various men around the bar. I knew if she drank them all she was going to be in trouble. I guess she knew it too because after just a short time she started passing them around the table.

When the band started playing Amy was approached immediately to go dance. I watched as Paul's expression fell. I leaned across the table.

"Go dance with her after this one."

"I'm not very good at dancing." He said.

"You don't have to be, just go have fun with her."

I had seen her looking his way and I knew she wanted him to ask her. Finally after a little prodding Paul went out to the dance floor.

Adam and I danced to a few songs but mostly we just sat around and watched everyone else. I think we were both tired from the night before and our early morning escapade.

Even though it was early I was ready to call it a night. I had just told Adam when Amy approached me.

"What are your plans for the rest of the night?" She asked in my ear, cutting her eyes over to Paul.

"I don't have any plans. Do you need the apartment empty?"

"Only if you can, If not he has a room."

I leaned over to Adam. "Mind if I stay another night?"

"Not at all, in fact I was hoping you would." He said with a huge grin.

I turned back to Amy. "I'll stay with Adam but I need to get some stuff."

Adam and I left then, him going to his apartment and me to get some clothes, and then go to Adam's place.

"Bring your gym stuff too if you want to go workout tomorrow." He said.

I arrived at Adam's, gym bag in tow. I had changed out of my dress into a pair of yoga pants and T- shirt. Adam had changed as well and was now wearing a pair of sweat pants.

Stowing my stuff in the room I came back out to the living room where Adam was watching TV. I settled next to him in front of the sofa and wondered briefly if either of us ever used a couch for more than a backrest.

Adam got up. "I'm getting a beer. You want one?"

"Yes please."

He came back with two opened bottles and handed me one.

"So what is the news you wanted to tell me?" I asked.

He sat down next to me again and shut off the TV.

"Mr. Jameson called me to his office today."

I waited for him to go on. I had only met Mr. Jameson once and he'd seemed like a nice man.

"He's talking of opening a small branch on Bainbridge and asked if I might be interested in a position there. It would mean a promotion and a salary increase."

"Oh," I said trying to take this all in. I really knew nothing about Bainbridge. "So would you have to move?"

"No I could just commute, although it would probably be easier to live there. The thing is it's not set in stone. If it happens it will be months away. I just wanted to tell you that's all."

I felt suddenly relieved. Despite the fact that this seemed to be a good opportunity for Adam, the thought of him moving away left me with a sense of panic. I knew I shouldn't feel this way but I did. I was in over my head with him after only a few days.

The fact that he was telling me this meant something too. This was a big step in his life if he were to take it. If he felt the need to include me in his decision what exactly did that mean? Was he in just as deep as me?

For whatever reason I suddenly thought about Joe and my inability to tell him I didn't love him. Without even noticing it I had somehow moved past that in just a few short days. Thoughts of him no longer triggered the pain I'd had before.

I knew for certain I was no longer in love with him. Being with Adam had helped me to get over him. But God help me if things didn't work out with Adam.

Reaching up I raked my fingernails across the stubble on his face. "It sounds like a great opportunity for you. I'm glad you told me about it."

He pulled my hand to his lips kissing each finger, his eyes never leaving mine. "I'm just glad you're here. That I had someone to tell."

We made love again and with each touch of his hands, each kiss from his lips I felt myself falling further and further past the point of no return. My body craved him like an illicit drug. He was my addiction and I couldn't get enough. I was falling into him; falling into Adam Knight.

More than once we fell asleep in each other's arms only to wake up and make love again. Already he knew my body better than I did and he used his knowledge to render me completely helpless against his sensual assault. We fit together so perfectly, like we were made for each other. But still I was afraid of waking up and finding it all just a cruel dream. Exhausted we finally fell asleep again and didn't wake up until well into the morning.

"Do you feel like going to the gym this morning?" He asked me.

I nodded. "But I could use some coffee first."

"Do you want to eat before or after?"

"After. I do better if I don't run on a full stomach."

Halfway through our workout Adam's phone rings. He pauses to wipe the sweat from his face before answering. He walks away a few feet while I finish my set. After a minute he returns.

"Hold on just a sec." He says into the phone. He pulls the phone away from his face looking at me. "It's my friend Davy. Would you mind going to his place for lunch? I've wanted you to meet him anyway."

"Sure." I agree. I had thought he was going to meet us the night before but something had come up.

Adam put the phone back to his ear. "We'll be there after our workout. About another twenty minutes."

He ended the call then sat down for his set of reps, talking to me as he did. "Gloria and Davy are both really nice people, but I need to warn you, she often says stuff that…well sometimes her mouth moves faster than her brain."

I laughed. "Okay." I said. "I am forewarned."

ELEVEN

Arriving at Davy's house, I looked around the yard as I walked up the short path to the front door. It was a small house in a nice subdivision with a well-manicured lawn.

It was not what I was expecting after hearing Adam's description of Davy. I guess I was half expecting something out of the Godfather.

Adam didn't even bother knocking; he just opened the front door and announced, "We're here."

"Great come on back to the kitchen," came the reply.

Adam placed his hand on the small of my back and guided me through the house to the kitchen where Gloria was busy making sub sandwiches.

Davy came around the bar and grabbed my hand. I recognized him immediately as being the man I'd seen playing basketball with Adam. He was a handsome man in his own way and my initial impression was that of Fonzy from re-runs I'd watched of "Happy Days".

"So good to finally meet you Drew," he said earnestly. "Adam here can't stop talkin' about you. Me and G- here were starting to think he was making you up."

Gloria came over wiping her hands on a dish towel. She was a pretty woman and well groomed. Completely made up from head to toe, she looked as though she'd just stepped from a fashion magazine. I felt bad just coming straight from the gym, not even getting to shower first.

She held out a manicured hand to me and offered a warm smile. "So nice to meet the girl who stole our Adam's heart."

"Nice to meet you too, I've heard so much about both of you."

Davy showed us to the dining table where Gloria placed a platter of sub sandwiches and chips. "I've got beer, sodas, and water in the fridge." He said. "What can I get you to drink?"

"I'll take a water please." I said.

"Beer here," Adam replied.

Once we were all seated Davy looked around the table. "So the reason I wanted you to come over is because G- and I have some news. It seems we're going to be having a baby in a few months."

Gloria smiled. "Yea," she said, "the condom busted."

"That is not true and you know it G-." Davy said.

"Alright, alright, I think maybe I bit a hole in it."

I laughed.

"Gloria!" Davy protested.

Gloria sighed. "That's not true eithuh. This is just what I get for lettin' him read 50 Shades of Gray."

Davy gave her a dirty look shaking his head. "The stuff I put up with!" He said in exasperation.

"What?" She said. "Can't we have a little humor?"

"Congratulations!" Adam said. "So when are you due?"

"End of March next year." Gloria announced.

Davy sighed. "Anyways, seeing as my mother and her father will kill us if we don't, we're planning to get married soon, before she gets too big. I'd like for you to be my best man." He said to Adam.

"Sure thing," Adam replied.

Gloria huffed. "You know we should just do this the fast way at the JP's office. You know I don't have anyone here to be my maid of honor."

Apparently this was not a subject that had been fully discussed yet.

"I told you," Davy said, "my cousin Denise can be your maid of honor."

"I'd rather have my Gran Mabel be my maid of honor than that cow cousin of yours."

"What are you talkin' about? Your gran Mabel is dead and buried."

"Exactly!" Gloria retorted.

"Oh we'll figure this out later." Davy said flustered. "Let's eat."

I smiled. This was better than dinner and a movie. Looking at Adam I could see he was enjoying the show too.

After lunch Adam and Davy walked out to the backyard. Gloria and I stayed at the table talking.

"So," I asked. "Are you excited about the baby?"

Gloria smiled. "Yea, I've just been a bit moody lately and this whole marriage thing has me in a frazzle. Don't get me wrong, I love Davy, I just wish it wasn't so rushed."

"If it weren't for our parents I'd say let's wait till after the baby is born and have a big wedding. I don't want to look like a fat cow walking down the aisle eight months pregnant."

I could see her point. "Maybe you could have it sooner, before you get big."

"I just don't know how I could get it put together fast enough. It's such a lot of work."

"I had a cousin who put one together in four weeks," I said, "but you're right, she was frazzled and grumpy the whole time. Of course there's always Vegas," I said grinning.

Gloria's eyes got wide at the suggestion, "Oh my god, why didn't I think of that? That would be just perfect. They have those little chapels and everything and Davy could have his best man." She sat quiet for a minute contemplating. "Say, you wouldn't want to be my maid of honor would you?"

I laughed. "Sure I guess, if I can get off work, anything for a trip to Vegas."

She raised her eyebrows at me. "Come on, let's go tell the boys."

Walking into the backyard she caught Davy's attention. "Listen, why don't we all fly out to Vegas one weekend, get married at one of those wedding chapels and stay the night at a casino hotel? Adam can be your best man and Drew will be my maid of honor."

"It'll be a lot cheaper and a lot faster than trying to plan a wedding and you can even have Elvis marry us if you want. And I won't have to have your cousin in my wedding. If we do it on a weekend you won't have to take time off work."

Davy looked at her thoughtfully for a minute. "Is this what you want to do?"

Gloria nodded.

"Okay then," Davy said, "we'll do it. But we are taking time off work for a real honeymoon. God knows we won't get to after the baby gets here."

Gloria squealed with excitement and hugged Davy around the neck. He smiled and kissed her pulling her close.

"Okay woman, I'll let you take care of the reservations. Just make sure we can get married once we get there."

Adam and I left shortly after that. Davy would call with details once Gloria made the reservations and booked flights. Gloria and I would get together one day soon to shop for a dress.

As we were pulling out of the driveway Adam took my hand in his. His expression was pensive as he kissed my fingers.

"Is something wrong?" I asked wondering about his mood.

He smiled then looking over at me, "No, nothing at all."

The following week went by quickly. We were extremely busy at work and had something to do just about every night after work.

Amy flittered around the apartment in a daze most of the time. She had it bad for Paul, who seemed to feel the same for her. She spent a good portion of every evening talking to him either on the phone or on Skype, whichever he could get to at the time.

They were making plans for his next break from school and were even talking of Amy going up for a weekend or two.

I stayed with Adam a couple of times and once he stayed with me, but that one time was awkward. Even though Amy pretty much kept to her room we still didn't have the freedom we had at Adam's. I needed my own place.

I told Amy that I was looking for an apartment. She understood. Besides I had a storage room full of stuff that I was starting to miss. I also had a feeling that Amy was going to need her privacy back soon.

When I mentioned it to Adam he seemed surprised. Then he suggested renting from his complex. I had already thought about it since it was close to both work and the gym. It also had easy access to the local market.

"You're sure you won't be uncomfortable with me living so close to you?" I asked. I didn't want things to get weird for him.

"Babe I'd be glad if you lived close by. I had even thought of asking you to move in with me, but I understand your need to be on your own for a while."

I was amazed at his confession. Did he really feel that strongly for me? I was glad he hadn't asked. I did need some time on my own. I applied at his apartment complex the next day.

Thursday evening Amy announced that she was driving up to see Paul for the weekend. She would be leaving from work Friday and already had her things packed and loaded into her car.

I invited Adam to stay the night and planned to cook some Texas style fajitas. I went to the market immediately after work Friday to get the stuff I needed. Amy had a small indoor grill that I could use to cook it on. I also picked up some Mexican beer and limes to go with it.

I stopped and checked the mailbox on the way in. My deposit refund check had finally come. Just in time too, I needed it for the deposit on the new apartment. I had opted for a one bedroom with a study. It was large enough for everything I had to put in it and I could use the study as a guest room if needed.

Adam was already at the apartment when I came in. He had brought clothes with him to work and I gave him the key so he could get in. I deposited the groceries on the counter then fixed us a couple of beers with lime and salt.

I heated the grill while I chopped the ingredients for pico de gallo and guacamole, opened a can of refried beans and seasoned the skirt steak.

In less than an hour we were sitting in front of the TV eating fajitas and corn chips with salsa. I was glad for a good piece of meat since I didn't have time to marinade.

Once again we were on the floor, using the sofa as a backrest. When I mentioned to Adam that we never used the couch he gave me a wicked grin.

"Maybe we can use it tonight. I can think of several ways to try it out. For that matter we could also use the dining table." He said, wagging his eyebrows at me.

Just having him talk about it was making me horny as I thought about having my breasts pressed against the glass of the table. A shiver went up my spine. I was ready for dinner to be over.

True to his word we did manage to find several ways to use the couch. Adam was in a playful mood tonight and I must admit I was enjoying myself immensely.

There was lengthwise on the sofa cushions; over the armrest; kneeling in front of the couch, and my personal favorite – over the back of the couch. For all its non-use, the couch truly got a workout.

Then we moved to the table, the island, and finally the shower. By the time we were done the only place untouched was the back porch. That was for obvious reasons.

Afterward we sat up late watching re-runs of "Big Bang Theory" on TV. I lay my head in Adam's lap and he began stroking my hair with his fingers.

"I love doing this kind of stuff with you." I said lazily.

His hand stopped for a moment then resumed its trek through my hair. "I…." He paused for a moment as if clearing his throat. "…love spending time with you too."

We went to bed and made love again, only this time is was slow and gentle. I straddled him as he lay on his back, him holding my hands as I slowly rode his beautiful cock.

With tender caresses he moved his fingertips down my arms to my breasts gently kneading them. My head fell back as I basked in the pleasure of his touch on my body.

My hands went to his face then his hair as my lips found his; our tongues dancing together in our mouths; our breath mingling.

I had fallen and I knew it. Fallen fast and fallen hard. There was no return from here for me, but it didn't matter. This was where I wanted to be. I hoped Adam wanted it too.

Adam lay awake long after Drew had drifted asleep in his arms. He liked listening to her breathe, liked feeling her skin beneath his fingertips. Liked…hell, who was he kidding, certainly not himself? He was in love with her; had been in love with her, almost from the very beginning. He had almost told her that tonight in the living room but was afraid of scaring her off.

The truth was she was everything he'd ever dreamed of in a woman. She was beautiful, funny, and smart. And they fit together so well, not just their bodies. The two just seemed to click.

He was comfortable around her and Lucy liked her too - so did Davy for that matter. Not that it would have made a difference but it was definitely a plus.

He had wanted to ask her to move in with him. Hell, last Saturday leaving Davy's he'd entertained thoughts of marriage. He knew he was moving too fast, but who made the rules anyway?

He didn't even really know how Drew felt about him. She had agreed to get to know him and she seemed to be enjoying herself with him, but what if this was just a fling for her?

He'd already ultimately embarrassed himself in front of her, but could he stand rejection? No he knew he would break if that happened. He was so afraid that it might.

She had admitted to still having feelings for her ex too. Suppose he came back into her life. Would she walk out of his life then? He shuddered and pulled her tight against his chest.

He shouldn't think about that. He should enjoy what he did have with her and hope for the best. After all, it was already more than he had thought possible.

With that he snuggled his nose into her hair and fell asleep breathing in her scent.

TWELVE

I was brought out of a deep sleep the next morning by someone pounding on the front door. I flew up in the bed, my heart instantly in my throat. Had something happened to Amy?

Adam was awake too as I jumped from the bed, scrambling to find some clothes to throw on. The pounding continued. Then I heard the voice.

"Drew, open the door. I know you're in there. Please I need to talk to you."

"Oh fuck! How the hell did he find me?"

"What? Who is it?" Adam asked, still in a state of confusion.

"It's Joe."

Adam sprang to his feet. "What the hell?"

I was afraid he was going to kick Joe's ass and he would have deserved it, but I didn't want any trouble for Adam.

"It's okay," I said trying to calm him. "Just let me go talk to him. It'll be alright. I promise."

Adam paced in the room, his fists clenching alternately with his jaw. He looked at me warily.

"Are you sure," he asked, a plea in his eyes.

"I'm sure," I insisted. "It will be okay."

"Alright, if this is what you want," he said, looking defeated. Something in his voice made me go to him. I stroked his hair.

"It'll be okay." I said again.

The expression on his face was one I'd not seen before, but I didn't have time to sort it out. Joe was beating the door down. The neighbors were bound to be pissed. It was Saturday morning and he was disturbing their sleep.

"Come on Drew, open the goddamn door." He yelled again as he continued to pound away against the layer of steel between him and me.

I flung the door open with Joe still pounding. He looked up surprised then took a step toward me with his arms outstretched. I stepped back.

"That's close enough Joe. What the hell are you doing here? I told you to leave me alone."

He stopped abruptly, awkwardly stuffing his hands into his pockets. "I needed to talk to you. You wouldn't answer my calls or my texts."

"I didn't want to talk to you. I thought I made that clear. What did you need to talk to me about that we haven't already discussed on the phone?"

"Can I come in?" He asked.

"No," we can talk right here."

He looked around suspiciously. "Is there someone in there with you?"

"That is none of your business Joe. Now what did you want?"

He stepped toward me again. "I want you Drew. I want you back. I need you back. I know I fucked up and I'm sorry. Look I drove all the way out here to prove it. Please give me another chance."

I stood staring at the man standing on my porch and for the first time I realized I didn't even know him. There was no place for him in my life now. I had truly moved on. The hurt had disappeared and had taken with it any feelings I'd ever had for him.

"I'm sorry Joe, but I can't. I've moved on and you should too now."

"But I drove all this way…"

I was instantly angry, my voice getting higher and louder as I spoke. "I stayed in Austin for six months Joe." I said cutting him off. "You could have saved yourself a trip to Washington at any point during that six month period but you didn't.

Joe suddenly turned ashen as I spoke and I thought I was finally getting my point across. Until I realized his gaze was fixed on an object over my left shoulder. His expression went from shocked to angry in two seconds flat. I turned to see Adam walking up behind me.

He was still clenching his fist and his eyes were stone cold, and shooting daggers at Joe. I had never seen Adam angry before and seeing him like this now sent a chill up my spine. This was not good. Joe I knew was a hot-head and right now Adam looked like he could kill him just for showing up on my doorstep.

"Are you okay Drew?" He asked never taking his eyes off Joe.

I started to answer but was quickly cut off. "Who the hell are you," Joe shot at Adam, "and what are you doing here?"

Adam looked at Joe coolly. "I'm Adam. I'm here because I was invited to be here by Drew. I stayed the night with her – in her bed – where we'd still be if some asshole hadn't disturbed us knocking the damn door down."

Fire flew from Joe's eyes as he bowed up ready for a fight. Adam was provoking him and he'd jump in feet first if I didn't do something to stop them. I knew Adam could take care of himself, but I still didn't want him or Joe to get seriously injured. I also didn't want them to destroy Amy's apartment. Quickly I moved between the two men.

"I'm alright Adam." I said turning to him. My eyes were pleading with him. I didn't want trouble for him. "Go back to the room." I begged. "I won't be much longer."

The look he gave me was icy as he turned and left the room. I watched as he went back down the hall then I turned back to Joe.

Joe was shaking his head. He still looked angry. "I guess that's the new guy." He said suddenly switching gears. "Look Drew, I know you say you're moving on but I think you still love me. You wouldn't get so mad if you didn't still have feelings for me. I wish you'd just admit it and we could move past this.

You don't need him. You need me. We were good together. We can be good again."

I shook my head not believing what he was saying. Where did this man come from? I'd certainly never seen him in the four years we lived together.

"Joe we were good together, but I wanted us to be great and you didn't want that."

My voice was low as I continued. I was finished with the fighting and I didn't want to upset Adam any more than he'd already been.

"I can't help that, after all these months, you've had a change of heart and think that you want me back. I've had a change of heart too. I don't need you and I no longer want you. Is that what you need to hear? I don't love you Joe. Now will you please, please… go back to Texas?"

He hung his head in defeat. "So you've really moved on?"

"Yes."

"And Adam…he's the one you want to be with?"

"Yes."

"Alright then, but if he ever leaves you…."

174

"Joe," I said shaking my head, "he's nothing like you."

We stood in awkward silence for long moments, his eyes pleading with me one last time. Finally he turned and walked down the stairs to his car. I watched after him as he got into his car and pulled out onto the road then drove off. I sighed. *Goodbye Joe.*

I didn't hate him. I hoped he could find someone that he could be happy with – really I did. It just wasn't going to be me. I shut the door, leaning against it for a minute, before making my way back into the bedroom.

Adam was sitting on the side of the bed completely dressed, staring out the bedroom window. His shoulders were slumped and he looked a bit pale. He looked up at me as I entered the room.

I was quiet, not knowing his mood. He had seemed so angry with me when he'd left me with Joe. I tried to study his face, but it was unreadable.

He sighed. "Well," he asked quietly, "what did you decide?"

"What do you mean?" I asked him, not understanding the question.

"About Joe…..are you going back to him? I just….I need to know."

The full force of what he was asking knocked the wind out of me. I suddenly realized the reason for his behavior earlier. *Did he really expect me to go running back to Joe?* My heart broke as I thought about the look I'd seen on his face when I left him in the room.

I couldn't stop myself. Going to him I knelt at his feet and wrapped my arms tightly around his waist.

"Never," I said, as tears began to slide down my cheeks.

Relief washed over his face as I looked up into his eyes. He pulled me from the floor, up into his arms and squeezed me so tightly it hurt. I straddled his lap and wound my arms around his neck as he kissed my face and neck.

"Does this mean I have a chance with you?" He asked between kisses, his eyes searching mine.

I cupped his face in my hands. "It means… please don't break my heart."

He pulled me close again, talking into my ear; his breath warm against my face, "I couldn't break yours without breaking my own." He said.

I was approved for the apartment lease and managed to get one on the ground floor just a few doors down from Adam. Over the next week Adam and I made trips to my storage unit picking up the small stuff that would fit in my car. I planned to rent a truck on the weekend for the furniture. The last stuff to be moved was what I'd brought to Amy's.

Davy contacted Adam with the dates for the trip to Vegas. It was two weeks out and Gloria and I still had not gone dress hunting. We would need to do that soon. I asked Adam if he had something to wear. He told me he had a nice black suit but could probably use a shirt and tie. I took down his size determined to find something that matched. I wouldn't choose my dress until Gloria had decided on hers.

My apartment was starting to look like home now. I was setting things up as I brought them in. My dishes and cookware were already in place in the cabinets. My coffee maker was set up and ready to go.

I was excited; I couldn't wait to make my first cup in my new apartment.

Early Saturday morning we picked up the truck from the storage facility, loaded my furniture and brought it to my apartment. Positioning the sofa in the living room I saw a smirk creep across Adam's face. He winked at me.

"Nice couch. We'll have to break it in soon."

I laughed thinking about our night of escapades at Amy's. After all the drama of Joe showing up that morning, Adam and I had made breakfast. He went to sit at the table and suddenly burst out laughing, motioning for me to come over.

There on Amy's glass table, big as life, were two hand prints. Several inches below them were the unmistakable imprints of two small breasts. My hand flew to my mouth and I started laughing too. There would be no way to deny what they were, and I damn sure couldn't claim they were Amy's. Thank goodness she always kept a bottle of Windex.

"Shame I don't have a table too." I said.

Adam looked around noticing for the first time. "Where are you going to eat?"

I pointed to the breakfast bar and the two barstools sitting next to it.

"That'll work." He said.

I would get the rest of my stuff from Amy's tomorrow. Today I was going with Gloria to look for a dress. Adam had plans for a game of basketball with Davy.

I rode with Gloria since I still didn't really know my way around Seattle. The only places I ever went were to work, home and the market.

The shop she wanted to look at first was on Bainbridge. This would be my first ferry crossing since coming to Seattle. I was excited for that reason, but also because Bainbridge was where Adam might work in the future and I wanted to see it.

The city was much larger than I had expected it to be, but the island itself was gorgeous. Gloria drove us around the outskirts of town so I got to see a little of both the city and the countryside.

We went to a tiny dress shop called Bernice's Fashions. Every square inch of the shop was packed with formal dresses. A sales associate named Alice greeted us at the door and within minutes had Gloria in the fitting room, trying on a selection.

I browsed around picking up a few different dresses, checking to see how much they cost. They all seemed to be reasonably priced.

Gloria called me back to the fitting area. She was trying a gorgeous floor length gown, a shade of green darker than mint, but not quite aqua. I decided it was a deep turquois; it looked great with her red hair.

She was beaming as she turned around to model it for me. She truly had a nice figure and looked lovely in the dress. If I could talk her into toning down her makeup a bit I could have her looking like a Greek goddess.

She was clearly in love with the dress. I hoped I could find something that would go well with it since I currently didn't own anything turquois. Once it was confirmed that Gloria wanted the dress Alice approached me.

"Will you be in need of my assistance today?" She asked.

I thought for a moment. "Possibly, do you think you could find something, not full length that would complement her dress?"

Alice studied me for a minute, tapping a finger on her lower lip. "I think I may have something. I want to try to work with the color of your eyes."

She left me and returned moments later holding two dresses. I couldn't believe anyone could find anything in here as tightly packed as the racks were but somehow she'd managed. Both dresses were knee length and both a darker shade of green that went well with Gloria's dress.

I tried the first dress. It fit perfectly but I didn't care for the style. The second one however was beautiful. I looked at the price tag. My recent move had depleted my funds and I hated spending unnecessary money.

It was affordable though and I justified it by telling myself I could wear it again, no alterations necessary - and I would. I had a pair of shoes, maybe two that would work so I was okay there, at least until Alice brought out the ones that went with the dress.

I have a terrible weakness for shoes so I simply don't go shopping for them unless I have to. That strategy keeps me from blowing my budget and keeps my credit card balance free. Alice must have seen me coming a mile away.

I was seriously struggling with myself over those shoes. I knew full well that the dress was already more than I needed to spend right now, and I still had to pay for my airfare to Vegas. Then Gloria just blurts out "We'll take them."

She smiled at me when she saw my face. "I'm paying for your dress and your shoes. You saved me a ton of money for my wedding and I don't have to stand by Davy's cow of a cousin. Not that I have anything against heavy people. I just can't stand her."

I couldn't believe it. "You don't have to buy my dress I protested."

"Nonsense, besides generally the bride pays for the dresses and I don't want you to feel bad about it."

That was hands down the fasted shopping experience I'd ever had. It had taken us little more than the drive time and we still had the entire afternoon ahead.

We stopped at the mall on our way back and quickly found a nice white dress shirt and a tie for Adam. The tie was multicolored containing the same shades of turquois as both of our dresses. I paid for those.

Once I got back I decided I had plenty of time to box up my stuff and finish moving. I really didn't have much, other that the clothes hanging in the closet. With the car loaded I returned to tell Amy bye.

She was on the phone with Paul, as usual, so I told him bye as well. They both promised to come see my apartment soon. Apparently Paul was coming into town to see Amy for a couple of days this week. I had made my move none too soon.

It felt awesome to be in my own place again. I kicked back on my couch and stared at my TV. My cable service wasn't hooked up yet so there was nothing to watch. It was just peaceful.

Getting up I went into the bathroom. I loved the garden tub and planned to use it soon. Most of the time I showered but still I liked the idea of being able to soak in a hot bath from time to time.

Realizing I had nothing to eat I decided to go to the market. I texted Adam telling him I would be at the new apartment tonight. He called me immediately.

"You're back already?"

"Actually I've been back. I just moved the rest of my stuff."

"That's amazing. My mom and sisters couldn't shop that fast."

"I laughed. We had an exceptional day. I need to go buy a few groceries now though."

"I'll come with you if that's okay. I need to get some stuff too."

"Sure, where are you?"

"Upstairs. I'll be right down."

I hadn't noticed his car in the lot but I guess I wasn't paying attention.

I'd barely hung up when he knocked on the door. I opened it with purse in hand and we left immediately for the store.

We shared a cart, walking up and down the aisles. I normally shopped with a list but I needed everything so a list wouldn't work. I made sure I grabbed a couple of toothbrushes. I wanted Adam to have one at my place and I'd leave one for me at his place.

Adam looked at the stuff in the cart. "You really cook don't you?"

I laughed, "Normally."

"Those fajitas you made the other night were really good."

"Thank you." I said wondering where this was going.

"Does everything you make taste that good?" I looked at what he had put into the cart; mostly boxed and canned items. I laughed again.

"Tell you what. Have dinner with me again tonight and you can judge for yourself."

"Okay, I'll get some wine to go with it then. What should I get?"

"White will be good."

We browsed the wine selection and he chose a chardonnay. Satisfied with his choice we went to the checkout.

I made parmesan crusted chicken, fettuccini and homemade Alfredo sauce with a tossed salad for dinner. Adam chilled the wine in a bucket of ice and poured us each a glass.

We sat together at the bar and ate dinner. Adam was thoroughly impressed with the food.

"I haven't had a home cooked meal this good since I moved out on my own - Except when I visit mom. Where did you learn to cook?"

"Sitting on the kitchen counter watching my mom. I've been cooking since I was a kid. When my mom went back to work I kind of had to take over that department."

"Really, how old were you when you started cooking."

"Eleven!"

I thought Adam was going to choke. "Wow, that's really young."

"Yea but it's just the way it was around the house. All of us kids had to do something to keep the household running smoothly."

"I don't remember either of my sisters really cooking." He said thoughtfully.

"My sisters didn't cook either," I said. "They just weren't interested. My older brother could cook pretty good though."

"Well, I'm glad you were interested. This is awesome." He said grinning. "I could get used to eating this good all the time."

I smiled playfully at him. "Well I can sure teach you some cooking skills."

He frowned. "That's not what I meant."

I laughed again. "I know. I'm just glad that you liked me before you found out I could cook. Otherwise I might have to wonder if it was me or the food."

We sat up talking and finished the bottle of wine then started another. I asked if he'd heard from Davy about the airline tickets.

"I took care of them." He said.

"How much was it? I need to pay you for it." I insisted.

"No you don't," he said. "It's taken care of and the room as well. I don't want you to pay me for it."

"You didn't have to do that you know. That's not why I'm with you, for you to pay my way." I said.

"I know I didn't have to, but I wanted to. Just like you didn't have to cook dinner for me but you did." He grabbed me around the waist and pulled me up into his lap.

"And I'm not hanging around just because I can get a real home cooked meal. It just happens to be one of the perks, and a damn good one I might add. I can give perks too." He said kissing me on the nose.

I leaned into his chest letting what he'd said soak in. I'd never thought about it like that before. "Okay," I conceded, "but just so you know. I don't consider the sex a perk, that's definitely something I'm hanging around for!"

Playfully he swatted my backside, and then with a wicked gleam in his eye said, "me too."

I showed Adam the dress I'd gotten for the wedding then I gave him the shirt and tie. He liked the tie and the fact that it went with my dress.

"Thanks for getting that for me." He said. "How much do I owe you for it?"

"Oh, it's just one of the perks." I said as I returned the dress to my closet.

He raised an eyebrow while wagging a finger at me. "You're not supposed to use my strategy against me." I just laughed.

Placing the shirt and tie on the foot of my bed he went to use the restroom. A moment later he emerged with the toothbrush I had bought for him. I had put it in a toothbrush holder and placed it on the vanity that I wasn't using.

"What is this for?" He asked leaning against the door jamb, holding it up for me to see.

"It's for you." I said, suddenly fearful that I may have overstepped my bounds by essentially designating an area in my apartment as his. "I just wanted you to have one here, if that's okay with you. If you're not comfortable….."

"Come here." He said cutting me off.

I moved cautiously toward him until I stood just inches away. Taking me by the arms he pulled me closer, lifting my chin until my eyes met his. I gazed into his deep blue pools of softness that were filled with unfathomable emotion.

My breath hitched in my throat. Being this close to him and the look in his eyes stirred a storm of desire inside of me. I couldn't get enough of this man.

I closed my eyes as he lowered his lips to mine. "It's more than okay." He whispered; his mouth and nose almost touching mine. I moaned, grasping his hair in my hands and closing the gap between us.

His mouth devoured mine, his tongue exploring and tasting my own as he emptied his emotion out into my very being. I melted into him, accepting everything he had to give; giving back from my own heart in return.

In a flurry of arms and legs we undressed each other, only breaking contact with our mouths when absolutely necessary.

"Wrap your legs around my waist." He commanded as he lifted me, pushing my back against the bedroom wall. I did as he instructed.

He braced one hand against the wall by my head. With the other he positioned himself at my opening, stroking me with the tip of his crown.

"Babe you are so wet! Are you ready for this?" He asked on a pant, placing his other hand on the wall.

I nodded. I was more than ready.

In one swift movement he pushed up and into me all the way to the root, filling and stretching me instantly.

"Oh God," I gasped at the sudden sensation of fullness.

Adam shook his head. "Oh, no baby, that's not God. This is all me and tonight I want you to feel me. In. Every. Inch. Of. You." He said punctuating each word. *Oh wow, I like this version of Adam too.*

He gave me a second to adjust to the fullness then began moving, pushing me a little further up the wall with each thrust. I pushed my head back against the wall; reveling in the pleasure he was bombarding my senses with.

"Open your eyes and look at me." He said. "I want you to see what I'm feeling; see how you make me feel."

My eyes locked on to his, my hands braced on his shoulders. Already I was spiraling up. This was just too intense. He pushed in again and I cried out. I wasn't going to last at this rate.

"Do you see it?" He asked. "See what you do to me?"

"Yes." I screamed as he pushed in again. I had seen it from the moment he called me over to him; felt it in his kiss; was overwhelmed, totally consumed by it now.

He thrust in again and I fell apart. "Adam," I screamed, "Oh baby, Adam," as my orgasm racked through my body."

"That's right baby," he groaned as he found his own release. "That's me, and don't ever forget it."

I knew I never would. Didn't think I ever could. He shifted me up a little and pulled me away from the wall. A few quick steps and we were collapsing into the bed together in a tangled heap of arms and legs.

I lie there in his arms trying to catch my breath. Thinking about what had just happened I started giggling.

Adam rolled up onto one elbow looking at me, rubbing my arm with his free hand.

"What is it you find so amusing Ms. Kosetty?" He asked; a smirk playing at his lips.

"Wow!" I said. "That was just…Wow, and all for a toothbrush. What would I get if I gave you a drawer?"

His eyes lit with that impish gleam he gets sometimes as he kissed me on the nose. "I don't know," he replied. "Give me one and we'll find out."

THIRTEEN

We had dinner at my place after work Wednesday night. Paul had come into town and since Adam and I would be leaving Friday midday, I wanted to spend some time with him and Amy.

We ordered Chinese delivery and I put some throw cushions around the coffee table to sit on since there were only two bar stools. No one seemed to mind. We all just sat around drinking Tsingtao and eating noodles.

I really liked Paul. As opposed to Matt who, in my opinion had never really fit with Amy, Paul was a good match for her. He was an attractive young man and very intelligent and I was truly happy for Amy. She deserved a good guy after putting up with Matt for so long. It was apparent that Amy was happy with Paul.

"So Ducky," Amy said. "Have you talked to your mom lately?"

I cringed and held my breath, hoping Adam hadn't noticed that little exchange. The look on his face told me he had.

"What did you just call her?" Adam asked.

I shot her a warning glance. She just waved me off.

"Ducky," She said. "That's what we used to call her in college. And don't think your dirty look is going to intimidate me." She said without missing a beat.

Adam grinned looking at me, talking to Amy. So where did you come up with a name like that?"

I was coloring all the way up my neck and face and he was immensely enjoying my embarrassment. This was no fair; two against one. I was going to kill her for this one.

She just smiled sweetly. It's an acronym I came up with from her initials - mostly. I glared at her which just fueled her on.

"Her initials," Adam asked. Paul was leaning in now, listening intently knowing he was about to hear something juicy.

"Her names," Amy replied, "Drusilla Unity Kosetty.

I buried my face in my hands and groaned as Adam looked at me with that impish grin. "I think it's cute." He says to Amy, still looking at me. He repeated my name. *God – someday I may kill my mother for doing this to me.*

"Drusilla Unity Kosetty." My face flamed even hotter if that were possible. "But that is only three letters. Where did the C and the Y come from?"

"Well it was actually Drusilla Unity Catty Kosette." Amy spouted off. "It was just Duck, but it didn't seem to fit that well so I stuck the Y on for good measure. Everyone loved it – except her of course."

My head was face down on the coffee table now as Adam threw back his head, roaring with laughter. "Catty, Tell me was she really catty in college?"

"Oh was she ever, but only once really," Amy said laughing. "After that all the girls were scared to death of her. Some girl had made a pass at Joe and this shy, timid little girl turned into a wildcat! I'd never seen anything like it in my life. It was so funny. They never messed with her guy again."

195

Adam was looking at me appraisingly now, but still had the smirk on his face. He raised his eyebrows at me, "Catty huh?"

"And don't you forget it!" I said looking at him coolly.

Adam laughed again then pulled me up into his lap and kissed me on the cheek. "I hope you'd be catty for me." He whispered in my ear.

My heart melted. If some other woman came around messing with him 'Catty' wouldn't begin to describe what I'd be.

I zipped the top of my duffle bag and brought it out into the living room. Adam's was sitting next to the door so I put mine with his. I had placed my dress as neatly as possible at the top of the duffle to avoid wrinkles. We would leave early from work and meet Davy and Gloria here then all ride to the airport together.

"Ready?" Adam asked as he pulled on a light jacket. It was starting to get cooler now as we moved through September.

"Ready." I said grabbing a cardigan off a barstool.

We had started riding in to work and to the gym together since I'd moved into the complex. Most mornings we woke up together as well, at one place or the other.

I had given him a drawer – actually the entire vanity after the toothbrush incident. Afterward I was rewarded with more awesome sex and a vanity of my own at his place. It definitely made things easier since we were constantly dressing for work at each other's place.

I stepped out into the chilly air and pulled my sweater tighter around me. I loved the cold air and bundling up for the winter, but having come from south Texas where we rarely had more than five days of winter weather, I had very few warm clothes. I would need to buy some before too long.

The morning seemed to fly by and before I knew it, it was time to leave. I gathered my purse and stopped at Amy's desk to tell her bye on my way out then went to meet Adam.

He was waiting by the bank of elevators when I rounded the corner and looked up smiling as I approached. On cue the elevator door opened just as I walked up and we stepped in together.

Someday I know that we will probably get busted for kissing in the elevator at work, but until that time we seem to be happy taking our chances. It's become our own little tradition.

FOURTEEN

We arrived at McCarran International Airport at four-thirty. Adam and I had only our carry-on bags to deal with but Davy and Gloria had to wait to collect theirs from the baggage pickup. It took a while for their stuff to come out so I flipped through a brochure while I waited.

Despite the fact that Gloria was pregnant, and therefore couldn't drink alcohol, I still thought she needed a bachelorette party. No matter how long she'd lived with Davy, it was going to be different once she married. She needed a last hurrah.

I'd racked my brains trying to come up with an idea and still had nothing. Then I spotted something on the last page of the brochure. 'Hunk Mansion' was the name of the place and it was not too far from where we were staying. According to the map, it was right down the street.

The wedding was scheduled for tomorrow at five p.m., anything we did would have to be tonight. I quickly programmed the number into my phone so that I could call for information once we got to the room.

The cab delivered us to the front door of the Bellagio. I'd had no idea what a nice place it was going to be and I was suddenly concerned about how much Adam had paid for our room. Surely I would have been just as happy at the Best Western right down the street, but I guess this was part of Gloria's plan.

Behind us some music started playing and I turned just in time to see a breathtaking display as the fountains began dancing with the music. We stood watching for a few minutes then turned to enter the lobby.

The lobby was enormous and very elegant with coffered ceilings and ornate tile flooring. I immediately wished that I had dressed a bit nicer as we made our way to guest services to check in. I stood quietly next to Adam as he collected our key cards then followed him to the bank of elevators.

He smiled at me as we stood waiting. "Our room is on the sixteenth floor." He said wagging his eyebrows at me. "We might have time for more than a kiss on that ride."

"Oh good," said Gloria as she walked up, hearing what Adam had said. "You hear that Davy? We might get to watch a show in the elevatuh." I laughed.

"Don't be ridiculous." Davy said walking up. "They don't have TV's on the elevators."

"Who said anything about TV? I was talking about live entertainment." She said winking at Adam and me.

Davy turned his brochure over. "I don't know where you get your information from." He said flipping through pages. "But there is nothing in here about live entertainment on the elevators."

Gloria winked at us again. "I like keepin' him in the dark; it gives me a sense of power." She said smiling.

Our rooms were on the same floor just a few doors down from each other. At the last minute Gloria had changed her mind about staying in one of the fancier rooms, deciding she would rather spend the money on the baby's room at home.

Adam opened the door to our room and ushered me in. I couldn't believe it. I had never stayed in a hotel room anywhere near this nice. It was hard to imagine they had some even fancier than this one.

Walking over to the window my hand went to the luxurious drapery. I was startled as the curtains suddenly started moving back on their own, revealing the sheer panels behind them and beyond a gorgeous view of the fountains. I turned to see Adam holding a small remote control, smiling at me.

"Well, what you think of the room?" He asked as I looked around.

"It's beautiful." I stated; setting my bag down on a chair. "Have you stayed here before?"

"Once…a few years ago."

I had to fight down the feeling of jealousy that invaded my thoughts as I wondered if he'd stayed with another woman back then.

He continued. "I was attending a business conference here. Funny the room I was in didn't seem that appealing to me at the time. But then I wasn't sharing it with a beautiful woman."

I was relieved but at the same time I knew I had to get over my petty jealousy. Adam had a life before me, just as I'd had one before I met him. No matter who he was with before, he was with me now and that was all that mattered.

Walking over I sat on the bed. "Oh wow! This is really nice." I said as I sank into the plush mattress. I lay back taking in the full effect. Adam came over and stretched out next to me.

"What do you want to do this evening?" He asked.

"You," I replied grinning.

He kissed me on the nose smiling, "And after that?"

"Umm, I think I could do you two or three times. That might hold me over till tomorrow." I said rolling over on top of him, straddling his hips.

He rolled his hips beneath me, "Only two or three times?" He asked with one eyebrow raised.

I laughed, leaning over kissing him. "Actually I thought maybe you could take Davy out for a while this evening and I could take Gloria. You know for a last hurrah, bachelorette type evening."

He ran his hands up and down my arms thoughtfully. "I was kind of thinking the same thing. Maybe grab something to eat first or we could meet up later and eat. What did you have in mind for Gloria?"

I smiled and wagged my eyebrows at him. "Oh, there's a place just down the road called 'Hunk Mansion' I thought she might have fun."

Adam frowned and narrowed his eyes at me, "Hunk Mansion huh? I'm not sure I want you being exposed to a bunch of hunky men in speedos. You might decide I'm not sexy enough for you anymore."

I thrust out my lower lip in a mock pout. Without warning Adam turned over, flipping me onto my back putting me beneath him. Pinning my hands up over my head he began a sensual assault nibbling and licking his way down my face and neck.

"Unless I mark my territory before you go." He said with a look of satisfaction that he had me exactly where he wanted me. "I could just give you something to think about; a little something to remind you of me when the hunks at the mansion are shaking their junk in front of you."

Being beneath him was my favorite place in the world. The weight of his body pressed into mine, holding me in place felt like heaven to me. There wasn't a hunk at the mansion that could make me feel the way Adam did.

But right now I was having fun with his possessiveness. "Humm," I said thoughtfully. "Maybe you'd better remind me before I go. I hear they have a lot of junk to shake around." I said with emphasis on 'a lot'

He bit my lower lip then holding both of my hands with one of his, snaked the other one down into the waistband of my pants. I closed my eyes as his fingers skimmed over the top of my sex.

"Do you need more than this?" He asked as his fingers pushed past the elastic of my panties.

I nodded. "Yes more."

He slowly moved his hand out of my pants up to my waist then slid beneath my shirt to my bra, "More than this too?"

That wicked grin of his had returned and was plastered across his handsome face. He was going to torture me and I was more than willing to lay here and let him. I could lie here for hours just looking at his dimple.

A sudden knock at the door followed by Gloria's Bronx New York accented voice had Adam rolling his eyes.

"What are you guys doing in there?" She called to us inside the room. I could just see her standing by the door with a face splitting grin, knowing she was harassing us.

"Are you guys doing it in there?"

"For Pete's sake G-, if they were doing it they're not anymore. Not with you bangin' on their door."

Adam got up off the bed and opened the door for them. Gloria walked in winking at him, Davy right on her heels.

"Boy Adam," she was saying. "You don't waste any time do you? Guess those books helped after all."

I laughed. "I thought about giving y'all something to listen to while you waited at the door. I started to fake an orgasm for you." I said as she walked further into the room.

"It wouldn't have worked." She said matter of fact. "I can tell a fake orgasm a mile away."

Davy shook his head while simultaneously rolling his eyes. "Now what the hell would you know about a fake orgasm?" He asked at her audacity.

"Everything," She replied. "I practically invented them."

Davy's mouth dropped open and his chin almost hit the floor. Adam and I were doubled over laughing so hard we had tears in our eyes. Poor Davy had walked right into that one.

Gloria gave us all a minute to laugh at Davy's expense before going to him saying, "But not with you babe. My orgasms are always real with you."

Davy shook his head. "I'm starting to think I should have come to Vegas without her."

Adam slapped him on the back. "Naw, you know you love her. And she's funny as hell." He said, his eyes twinkling.

I finally stopped laughing long enough to catch my breath. "Adam is taking you out tonight and I'm taking Gloria with me."

"Good take her." He said, still a little hurt. "Where are you going?"

"We're going to the 'Hunk Mansion.'" I stated.

Davy's eyes almost bugged out of his head, "The Hunk Mansion?"

"Don't worry." I assured him. "I won't let anyone molest her."

Davy huffed. "I'm not worried about her being molested. I'm more worried about the guys."

Gloria smacked him on the shoulder. "And for good reason, it's been a while since I saw a real hunk...except for Adam here." She said winking at Adam. Once again Davy rolled his eyes. He just couldn't win a battle of wits against Gloria.

We decided to grab a quick snack then meet up later for a real dinner. I think the guys just didn't want us with the 'hunks' for too long, but I figured a few hours of men in speedos were about all I could handle anyway.

Sharing a cab, we rode to the Mansion and left the guys to go do whatever it was they had decided on. Honestly I didn't even want to know.

Gloria informed me on the way in that her doctor had told her she could have a little alcohol and she was planning to have one drink tonight. She had not had any since she found out she was pregnant three months ago.

As always she had dressed to kill but tonight instead of her usual colorful eye shadows she was wearing smoky blacks. She was still just as thin as the day I met her, not even a tiny bump to indicate she was pregnant.

She was wearing a pair of black, skinny pants with a silver 'pirate' style top that hung off of one shoulder and a pair of black and silver, platform sandals. She had arranged her red curls to frame her face without clips. The only thing she wore in her hair tonight was the tiny bridal veil I'd given her for her bachelorette status. She looked really good.

We could hear women screaming riotously as soon as we got out of the cab. Gloria looked eager to go inside and see what it was all about. Secretly I had purchased a male revue for her. This was supposed to assure her one on one attention from one of the dancers.

As soon as we walked through the doors we were greeted by one of the 'hunks' who took Gloria by the hand and led her to a seat. I followed behind and sat next to her. She was then offered a shot of alcohol but she declined saying she preferred a mixed drink to sip on for a while.

She was beside herself with glee, almost drooling as the man started dancing for her, tearing away his clothing. In no time she was right up next to the stage cheering him on and stuffing money into his pants. He was HOT and I was enjoying the show too, but mostly I enjoyed watching Gloria's reaction to him.

It wasn't too difficult for him to figure out that Gloria was not shy and he soon had her up on the stage with him. At that point she started stuffing the money in her own pants and top, having him remove it with his teeth. He seemed to be having as much fun as she was, having her slide her hands all over his bare flesh. I made sure to take a lot of pictures.

She was screaming at the top of her lungs now, laughing and carrying on with her hunk. He was stripped all the way down to his speedo now. Suddenly he grabbed her and laid her back on the padded stage, moving between her legs that were up in the air. She was squealing with delight.

"Is there something extra special I can do for the bride-to-be tonight?" He asked her as he nuzzled close against her body in a sexual pose.

"Oh my God," she yelled in a fit of giggles. "Please tell me you'll be my baby's daddy."

Hunk just smiled and dipped low, snagging another bill from her bra with his teeth. It was then that I realized she had bills stuffed everywhere. She had them behind her ears, in her bra straps, bra cups, waistband, pockets, zipper, leg openings and even some hanging out of her shoes.

I couldn't stop laughing as I snapped away with the camera in my phone. She was having the time of her life and I hoped she never forgot tonight. I knew I never would. The sight of her with money hanging out everywhere would go with me to my grave.

She was breathless and still giggling when we left the building later that evening. Not one single bill had been left. Her hunk had removed each one in a slow tortuous manner with his teeth.

"Just how much money did you have stuffed in your clothes for him to take out?" I asked curious.

"Two hundred dollars," she said with a grin. "And it was worth every damn penny."

We were in the cab headed back to the hotel when Gloria turned to me, a frown of concern on her face. "You won't say anything to Davy about how I was acting tonight, will you?"

I shook my head, "Of course not! Hoes before beaus' right?"

Gloria smiled, "See, I knew I liked you!"

We met Adam and Davy back in the hotel lobby and went from there to eat. Davy was so wasted he could barely stand up without Adam holding him. Adam just grinned when I raised my eyebrows at him.

"What are friends for," he asked, "if not to buy you another round?"

"Damn it." Gloria blurted. "The one night I need him fully functioning and he gets sloshed."

Adam looked at her, puzzling over her statement.

"After two hours with those hunks at the mansion I'm just about to blow. I need to let off some steam." She said, answering his unspoken question.

This time it was Adam's turn to raise an eyebrow.

"What are friends for?" I said meeting his gaze. "If not to take you out for the time of your life and never tell anyone what you did while in Vegas."

FIFTEEN

It was noon before I woke the next day. The room was still perfectly dark thanks to the wonderfully thick drapes over the windows. Adam lay sleeping next to me.

It had been a fun night. Despite Davy's drunken state we had drug him all over town, forcing water down him every chance we got in hopes that he would at least partially recover before tonight.

I drank very little, not wanting to deal with a hangover today. Still it had been almost four o'clock when we finally made it back to the room; five when we got in bed.

Gloria was a riot to hang out with. She was a natural born smart-ass and had something funny to say about everything. Poor Davy had been the butt end of her jokes several times but it was all in good fun and never degrading.

The alcohol seemed to bring out Davy's creativity too and he had a comeback for most of her jabs. Still, watching them interact, it was apparent how much the couple cared for each other. Several times I looked up to see Gloria gazing at him with a look of pure adoration. I knew they would be great together.

Adam stirred and I moved closer to him, kissing him lightly on the forehead.

"Hey, are you feeling okay this morning?"

He groaned. "Not as good as I'd hoped. I think I'm still drunk."

"I'll get you some water." I said climbing out of bed. I turned on the bathroom light. I'd brought some Alka-Seltzer just for this occasion.

It took me a minute digging around in my bag to find them then I grabbed one of the cold waters out of the fridge. Pouring it into a glass I dropped in the tabs and brought it to Adam.

He sat up on the side of the bed. "Thanks." He said taking the drink from me. He drank it all and I poured him some more water, encouraging him to drink that as well.

He rubbed his hands over his face. "Remind me not to drink that much again." He said attempting to stand up. He teetered to one side and I grabbed him, putting his arm around my neck to steady him.

"I'll try." I said. "You need the bathroom now?"

"Yes please."

I helped him into the bathroom where he steadied himself leaning against the toilet. I turned the water on in the shower to heat up for him and then helped him undress.

Helping him into the shower I undressed and got in behind him. I didn't want him to fall in the shower as unsteady as he still was. I washed his hair then went to work on the rest of him while he stood under the hot water.

Once done I helped him out and toweled him off. By the time I finished, the water and Alka-Seltzer was starting to work and he was able to stand up straight to dress by himself. I got dressed then giving Adam another bottle of water, pulled him out the door to get some breakfast.

We ran into Gloria in the hall on the way. Davy had had a rough go of it, spending a few hours kneeling at the porcelain throne before he finally went to sleep. She was going to eat and bring some food back for him. With any luck he'd be able to eat by the time she got back.

Adam still wasn't hungry but I made him eat a few bites of egg, knowing it would help his queasy stomach. I packed a bagel for later when his appetite came back.

It was two-thirty by the time we got back to the room. Davy was up moving about and Gloria was visibly relieved. We had only two and a half hours before the wedding.

After Davy ate his breakfast, Gloria brought her dress to our room to get ready for the wedding. Adam went to change in their room. We would meet the men at the wedding chapel at four-thirty.

"Tell Davy don't forget the marriage license." Gloria said to Adam as he left.

He was feeling better, eating the bagel I'd brought back for him. He nodded and waved; his mouth full of bagel.

At four-thirty sharp our cab delivered us outside the chapel. The men were nowhere in sight and we were quickly ushered into one of the side rooms where an attendant came in to go over the details with us. She told us when to walk, where to stand and where the photographer would be as we entered.

Just as she was finishing we heard music starting over the sound system. It was the song Gloria had chosen for her wedding march.

"It's time." The attendant said as she led us out the door and around to the chapel entrance. She sent me in first and I walked down the aisle, taking my place across from Adam. He looked so handsome in his black suit standing next to Davy.

Davy was looking a bit nervous, glancing down the aisle several more times after I came in. Leaning over he whispered something in Adam's ear. Adam's eyes met mine with a look of concern. I gave him a small smile and nodded. *Yes she is here and yes she still wants to marry him.*

Adam then shook his head and I saw Davy visibly relax. A moment later the music changed and Gloria appeared at the entrance. Then slowly she made her way towards us.

She was beautiful in her long dress and I think I saw Davy wipe back a tear. Her hair was swept up in a loose knot with curls falling everywhere, framing her face.

She had allowed me to apply her makeup so I had used greens and creams that matched her dress for her eyes and wine colored lipstick with nude gloss.

When she stopped at the end of the aisle she was positively glowing. Davy looked awestruck as he went to stand next to her. Taking her hand he brought it to his mouth and kissed her fingers.

I looked across at Adam only to find him looking at me instead of the bride; his expression reverent. For just a moment my heart stopped beating in my chest and I transcended time and space. It was just the two of us in the room as our eyes met and held, and unspoken words passed between us.

Then I saw Gloria move and I stepped forward to accept her bouquet while the couple exchanged rings. Taking their places in front of the minister the couple exchanged vows facing each other.

When the minister pronounced them husband and wife, Davy surprised Gloria by dipping her almost to the ground, kissing her passionately. I was cursing under my breath that I didn't have my camera. Fortunately Adam did and was on the spot for the candid shot.

We all went out for dinner and a show afterward then stayed out late dancing. I had danced with Adam before but never ballroom style. He was an excellent dancer and I was able to follow his lead with ease.

"Where did you learn to dance?" I asked him as he was spinning me around the dance floor.

"My mother made me take lessons when I was younger, for five years from the time I was ten. Learning to dance was something she insisted for all of us kids."

"I really hated it and resented her for it for a while, until my first school dance when I realized I could do something the other guys couldn't, and the girls loved it."

"That night after the dance I was the talk of the school when a football jock busted my lip for dancing with his girl." He grinned fondly at the memory.

"You must have been very proud of that dance." I said picking at him.

He just laughed. "Actually I was proud of making a football jock jealous. That was one of the few times in my life where I wasn't a wall flower around girls."

At two a.m. we make our way back to the hotel. Davy and Gloria will be staying on for several more days but Adam and I are flying back to Seattle tomorrow at noon.

"Did I tell you how beautiful you look tonight?" Adam asks, wrapping his arms around me from behind.

"Umm, maybe once or twice," I say smiling.

He turns me around in his arms to face him. His eyes are deep blue pools, filled with longing. Lowering his lips to mine, he slowly begins to plunder my mouth with his tongue, tasting, exploring.

I surrender completely, my body melting into his as he pulls me closer, his erection evident against my belly.

Pulling his head back he looks into my eyes again.

"I want to make love to you Drew. Let me love you."

I nod, pulling his head down to kiss him again.

Slowly he trails his lips down my face and neck in a sensual assault. He stops only long enough for him to unzip and remove my dress and then continues down my body with his mouth.

Stepping back away from me he leaves me standing with nothing on but my bra, panties and shoes. His eyes never leave my body as he removes his suit coat, tossing it across a chair, and then his tie.

His hands move to his cuff links then the buttons on his shirt as I unhook and remove my bra, dropping it on the floor. I'm breathing harder now, eagerly awaiting his next move.

His eyes remain on me as he unbuckles his belt, pulling it smoothly from the loops of his pants. I stoop and remove my shoes, one then the other. He begins to move toward me again.

My hands go to the waistband of my panties. Adam continues slowly toward me shaking his head.

"Leave those for me." He says kicking off his shoes, his gaze still locked onto mine.

My mouth is suddenly dry and I lick my lips to moisten them as he comes to stand directly in front of me. His shirt is completely unbuttoned, hanging loosely exposing his beautiful chest and abdominal muscles.

I reach up touching his face feeling the day's growth of beard on his jawline. Covering my hand with his own he leans into my touch, closing his eyes for a moment. He then moves his hands, wrapping his arms around me, pulling me close against him.

"I've waited all day just to have you to myself." He whispers into my hair.

I wrap my arms around his waist beneath his shirt, relishing in the feel of his muscles beneath my fingertips and the scent of Adam. My hands glide slowly up his back, over his powerful lats then back down his spine.

I feel his muscles ripple beneath my hands and then he's lifting me, carrying me across the room to the bed. Flinging back the covers with one hand he deposits me gently onto the mattress and once again steps back.

He shrugs his shirt off his shoulders then removes his pants and socks. I'm panting in anticipation. The hunks at the mansion had nothing on this man.

Closing the distance between us he moves onto the bed between my legs, pushing me back as he advances. Our mouths connect and I fall the rest of the way onto the bed, taking him with me as our tongues dance slowly together.

He pulls back nipping my lower lip between his teeth before descending to my neck, kissing and licking a gentle path to my breasts, suckling them tenderly.

I'm overwhelmed with emotion and the desire for him to take whatever he wants or needs from me. There is nothing I'll withhold from him. Nothing I wouldn't do right now.

My hands go to his head as my body arches into his and I hear him moan against my breast.

"Oh baby, please." I beg. He's not even touched my sex and still I'm flooded with desire. I need him.

His refusal to move any faster is pure agony. I need him, like an addict going through withdrawal I crave him. He is the one thing that can satisfy my hunger but he's withholding himself just out of my reach. I want him closer...want him inside me, and not having him is causing me mental and physical anguish.

"What do you want baby?" He asks. "Tell me what you need."

"I want you." I whisper. "I need you."

Kneeling up he removes my panties and slides a finger inside. I hear a sharp intake of air. "Oh baby." He moans as he starts to pump his finger inside me.

The pleasure is incredible. My head pushes back into the mattress as I push my hips against his hand. The anticipation alone has pushed me to the edge of orgasm. It won't take much to send me flying.

He removes his hand and I watch as he takes off his boxers; his erection hanging impressive and heavy from the surge of blood it's receiving. My eyes worship his beautiful body between my legs.

I continue to watch as he lowers his mouth to my sex, lapping at the entrance to my body. Sucking and nipping on my clit. His fingers are inside me again working their magic.

"Baby your pussy is so sweet. I love the way you taste."

I groan and push against him, seeking out more friction. I'm on the verge of explosion and want more of him. My fingers pull in his hair.

"Baby please, I can't wait any longer."

"Is this what you want?" He asks rising up on his knees. His beautiful cock gripped firmly in one hand.

"Yes you, all of you." I needed him inside me – Now.

"Then baby, that's what I'm going to give you." He says as he pushes inside me.

The feeling is exquisite as he fills me again and again. I meet him thrust for thrust pushing hard against him. I want him buried deep inside me. I need this connection.

"Yes." I scream. I'm breaking apart inside. Now that I have him here I never want to let him go.

Then suddenly I can't hold back any longer. In cathartic release I cry out loudly calling his name, tears pouring from my eyes, running back into my hair.

As my orgasm explodes around him Adam finds his own release moaning my name as he continues to pump until he's emptied completely inside me. Spent he collapses down on top of me.

I'm still sobbing, unable to stop the tears that continue unbidden.

"Baby are you alright? Did I hurt you?" He asks concerned.

I shake my head. "No." I say with broken breaths. "I'm okay."

"Why are you crying baby? Please tell me. Did I do something wrong?"

I shake my head, wiping the tears from my eyes.

"Please baby." He pleads once again. "I need to know why you're crying."

I don't know what to say to him. He has done nothing to hurt me or cause me grief. The intensity of my feelings for him, combined with my need to have him swell inside me until I think I might burst open. The result is tears. I've never experienced an orgasm quite like this. Never felt release in such a way that bound me to someone before.

Pulling him down to me I kiss him pouring everything I have into it; willing him to experience what I feel. When I release him he still looks concerned.

"I just need to know that you're okay, that I didn't hurt you baby."

"You didn't hurt me Adam." I reply. "I...It's just that...I love you."

I'm afraid for a moment how he is going to react to me dropping the L-bomb on him. It's all so fast, but I can't help it. I am hopelessly in love with him.

He pulls me tight into his chest, rolling over so that we are next to each other, facing one another. His eyes are moistened with tears. Then he kisses me again slowly, tenderly delving into my mouth with his velvet tongue, consuming me with his passion. Pulling back he holds me in his gaze, stroking my face with his knuckles.

"I love you too baby. I think I always have," he says. Then he kisses me again.

We made love again, me astride him, riding his beautiful cock before finally falling asleep entwined with each other. Oddly enough my last thoughts were of Joe. In those moments just before sleep all I could think of was how thankful I was that he had left me when he did.

SIXTEEN

The sound of the landing gear squawking on the tarmac woke me up. I had leaned my head against Adam's shoulder and must have dozed off. I was exhausted. Neither of us had gotten much sleep the night before.

Adam squeezed my hand. "Not too much longer baby and I'll have you home in bed. I know you need some sleep."

"You look like you could use some too." I noted. "You were up just as late as I was." His eyes sparkled remembering the night before.

"I would stay up for a week just to hear you tell me what you did last night too." He tucked a stray strand of hair behind my ear, caressing my face with the back of his hand.

The captain announced that we could begin exiting the plane momentarily. Adam collected our bags from the overhead compartment and helped me to my feet.

We made our way down the concourse then out of the airport. I was surprised at how much cooler it had gotten since we'd left just two days ago. I pulled my sweater tighter around me. Adam noticed and stopped to remove his jacket.

"I'm alright." I told him. "Let's just get the car."

I couldn't put off buying some winter clothes much longer though. Maybe I'd make a trip to the mall after work tomorrow. Adam wrapped his arm around my shoulder and we headed to the car.

It only took us a few minutes before we reached it and Adam quickly opened the door for me and helped me inside. Going around to the driver's side he slid behind the wheel and started the car.

It was a quiet ride home; both of us seemed to be lost in thought. As much as I enjoyed the weekend I was glad to getting back to my own place and my own bed.

Adam pulled up in front of my apartment and shut the car off, not moving for a minute. Finally he turned to me.

"You haven't changed your mind about me have you?" He asked, a frown furrowing his brow.

"Not at all, why do you ask?" I asked taking his hand.

His expression was serious when he turned to face me. "It's just that I've never felt like this about anyone before and I've suddenly realized how bad it would hurt if you ever stop loving me. Please don't ever stop loving me Drew."

My heart crumbled. How could I ever stop loving him? Tears filled my eyes as I pulled him to me.

"Don't ever stop loving me either."

We spent a quiet evening drinking a bottle of wine and eating cheese while soaking in the bath tub. As cool as the air was outside now the hot water felt great.

Getting out of the tub we ordered Chinese delivered and ate dinner at the coffee table, leaning against the couch. Adam twirled some noodles around his fork. His face contorted into a frown, like he was trying to remember something.

"What is it?" I asked wondering what was on his mind.

"I was just thinking." He said as he continued to twirl his noodles. "That we never did properly break-in this couch." He took a bite of his noodles and wagged his eyebrows at me.

My body flushed and warmed at the thought. As tired as I was, I was still instantly aroused by the memory of our last romp on the couch at Amy's. My fork stopped halfway to my mouth. I was suddenly flooded with desire and eating was no longer a priority.

Adam leaned close. "Eat your dinner baby. You're gonna need your strength for what I've got planned for you." He said with a smirk playing in his eyes.

I wondered if he knew just how much he affected me. I stuffed the last few bites of food in my mouth quickly cleaning my plate.

"Okay," I said smiling up at him. "I'm ready for desert!"

Adam leaned back against the sofa eating his dinner next to Drew. This had become so normal and second nature to him that he couldn't imagine her not being with him.

Being with her pushed him to his physical limits and beyond though. Just being near her kept him in a constant state of arousal and it took nothing for him to get a hard on. Even when he was exhausted his body would still respond to her. That was something he'd never experienced with anyone else.

Since their confessions the night before Adam could hardly think of anything but getting her in bed beneath him again. The thoughts of pushing his cock into the wet warmth of her pussy; the taste of her beaded nipples against his tongue were pushing him over the edge.

He loved that they were together almost every night, but he wanted it to be permanent. He wanted Drew to understand that she was his and that he was hers alone. He wanted to go to sleep with her every night and wake up every morning with her.

Already he had a hard on thinking about her as he swirled his noodles around on his fork. The things he wanted to do with her and that firm body. The positions he wanted to put her in as he pumped his hard cock into her tight pussy.

He knew they both had to work tomorrow and he wished they'd taken off a few days more. He'd like nothing better than to spend an entire day in the bed with her, making love and lounging around.

Still he'd make use of the time they did have and try to get her to bed early so she could rest before work tomorrow. Looking at her now, and the way she was looking at him, he couldn't make any promises.

I woke the next morning with Adam's arms and legs draped across me. We had fallen asleep that way after a romp on the sofa that was continued into the bedroom. Coming loudly, he collapsed down on top of me then proceeded to cover my face with kisses.

"I love you baby." He had said, still breathing hard against my neck.

"I love you too, Adam." Tears once again threatening as I held him tight against me.

Disentangling myself from his arms I went to use the bathroom. I winced as I lowered myself onto the toilet. I was sore from all the sex we'd had the last two nights.

It was still early. My alarm wouldn't go off for another half hour so I decided to soak in a hot bath.

Turning the water on I went to my closet and laid out the clothes I would wear today, including one of the few sweaters I owned. I needed to go after work and shop for some winter clothing.

As I lowered myself into the foamy liquid the heat began soothing immediately. I began to relax and must have dozed off. I awoke with Adam kneeling next to the tub.

"Are you alright baby," He asked; concern etched his voice.

I smiled and stroked his face with my hand. "Yes, just a little sore that's all."

He kissed my forehead. "I'm sorry baby. I kept you up too late. I should have let you sleep last night."

"I'll get in bed early tonight. I need to go buy some winter clothes after work so I can just pick up something for dinner on my way home."

Adam frowned. "How about if I drive you and when you're finished shopping we stop for dinner? We could leave from work and get you home early for bed."

"Are you sure you want to hang out at the mall with a girl?" I grinned.

"Positive." He kissed me again and helped me up out of the tub, wrapping me with a towel.

"I don't need a lot. I just don't want to get caught without a coat when it gets cold."

We ate a quick breakfast and made our way to work. I kissed Adam goodbye as I got off on the fifth floor and went to my desk. Another Monday and I was too tired to be here but with any luck it wouldn't be a bad day.

Amy came in just moments later and I noticed right away something was different about her. She rolled her chair over to my desk and sat grinning from ear to ear. I arched an eyebrow at her.

"Spill it." I demanded. "I want to know why you have that shit eating grin on your face."

She wasted no time. "I think I'm in love." She said, her eyes swimming with joy.

I was shocked. The Amy I knew would never admit to that after only a few dates. Hell she never even really claimed to love Matt and she'd asked him to move in with her. She must have seen the surprise on my face because she quickly began to talk again.

"I know, I know. This is Amy here. The one that keeps men at arm's length and pushes for total

236

independence, but Paul is the one. I've never felt more right about anything in my life."

I didn't quite know what to say. Finally I hugged her. "I'm so happy for you Amy. So tell me what all has been going on. I was only away for a weekend."

"It really started the first night we met. It was just…electric, and we get along so well. We talk every night and spend as much time together as possible. He wants me to consider moving in with him as soon as he's out of school. Of course it may mean making another move, depending on where he gets his internship"

"How soon will that be?" I wondered aloud.

"End of May next year. I think I'm going to do it Ducky. I really think I'm ready for this. I just can't imagine living without him."

I smiled again. I was truly happy for her although if she moved I was going to miss her.

"So tell me about your weekend." She said sheepishly. "I was just coming down from the break room, putting up my lunch when I ran into *Dark and Dangerous*. He looked like the canary that ate the cat so I know things must be cooking with him"

I laughed at her name for Adam, knowing it was from the book Davy had given him to read. I leaned in closer.

"The weekend was awesome. The wedding was perfect and… I told him I loved him."

Amy's eyes got big as saucers. "Ohmygod!" she said bouncing in her chair. "What did he do? What did he say to that? He must have been okay with it 'cause he was all smiles this morning."

Her excitement was contagious and it was bubbling over onto me. "He said he loves me too." I whispered, unable to contain my exuberance.

I was caught off guard by the intrusion of another voice into our conversation. It was Ned, "Well isn't that sweet," he said facetiously. "Sounds like it could be an HR violation to me."

Amy shot him a dirty glance. "Who spit in your bean curd this morning?" She spat at him. "Adam didn't interview her, didn't hire her, and he doesn't sign her paycheck. So since there is no company policy against employees dating or marrying there is no HR violation."

Ned slid back down behind his partition, but I wondered what his problem was. What should it matter to him that I was dating Adam.

Amy squeezed my hand. "Let's do lunch today and we can talk more."

"Alright," I agreed.

I texted Adam to tell him I was having lunch with Amy. A few minutes later I got his text back.

Adam: *ok babe. C U after work.*

At lunch time, rather than eating on the roof, Amy and I opted to eat at the bistro just down the block. It was a bit nippy out so we ate inside. We had a lot to catch up on since I'd moved out and I'd missed sitting around talking to her.

I made a point to spend more time with her while she was still around. We were both busy with our relationships but we could at least do lunch more often.

"Why do you suppose Ned is so angry about me and Adam dating?" I asked when we were seated.

"Isn't that obvious Ducky?" She had started calling me that again but for some reason it just didn't bother me anymore. Adam called me Ducky too from time to time.

I frowned. "No, I mean he seems to be jealous of Adam for some reason but I don't see why."

Amy lowered her head and cut her eyes up at me. Her fingernails strumming on the wooden table top. "How many times did Ned ask you out before you started seeing Adam?"

"I don't know...a lot. Maybe five or six...Oh" I said, realization dawning on me. "So you think it's because of me?"

"Yep," Amy stated matter of fact.

I could see why she would think that, but at the same time it just didn't seem to be a sufficient reason. After all it wasn't like I had left him for Adam. I had never even gone out with him. Something just didn't seem right but I let it drop. It really didn't concern me anyway.

Adam and I left work that evening and drove out to the mall. It was even cooler than it was this morning and I pulled my sweater tighter around me. Adam wrapped his arm around my shoulder and ushered me into the mall entrance.

Out of the wind it was much warmer and he released my shoulders and took my hand, twining our fingers together. As we made our way to the store

I planned to shop at, I stopped to admire a pair of boots in the window of one of the many shoe stores.

I hadn't planned on buying boots today and since shoe stores were taboo for me I decided to pass on them and get the stuff I really needed at the moment. Although a pair of boots would be sensible when the weather turned really cold.

Adam left me at the entrance of the store allowing me time to shop while he went to check on some things. I told him I'd text him when I was ready to meet him.

On my way to the women's department I had to walk through men's wear and found myself shopping for Adam. I found a very nice gray and blue sweater that I decided would go great with his eyes and another solid black one. Then I made my way to the women's section.

I had several light jackets but I needed a real winter coat. I found a wool Pea coat and a couple of sweaters that would go with my skirts and pants then went to find some leggings to wear under my skirts.

I texted Adam when I got to the register. He replied that he would meet me at the entrance where he'd dropped me off.

I had to wait a couple of minutes before I saw him walking up with two large bags, one in each hand.

"You did some shopping yourself I see."

He smiled. "I got a few things. You ready to go eat?"

I nodded. He reached to take one of my bags from me when we reached the mall exit.

"You might want to put on your coat now before we leave. I think the temperature has dropped some more since we got here."

He was right so I took the tags off of my new coat and put it on. It was more coat than I needed but at least I wasn't freezing. We stored the rest of our purchases in the trunk then went to eat.

We made it back to the apartment around eight and brought our purchases in. I was eager to show him the sweaters I bought for me as well as the ones I'd gotten for him.

To my surprise he presented me with a large box containing a pair of the boots I'd seen in the store window. I loved them and they fit perfectly. They were black leather and came all the way up to my knees. I was ecstatic.

"How did you know my shoe size?" I asked amazed that they fit.

"I know what size you are with just about everything." He said with an impish grin. Holding his hands down in front of him like two C's facing each other he stated, "Your waist," then spreading his hands further apart, - "Your hips." And then turning his palms up in a cupped fashion, - "Your boobs."

I laughed. "I guess you've got it down to a science then. What did you use for my foot?"

Taking one of the boots from me he sat the heel on his shoulder, toe pointing up, measuring where the toe was next to his head. "I figured this was pretty close."

"Uh-uh, tell me you did not do that in the shoe store."

He pulled me close and kissed me laughing. "No, I'm just messing with you. I do pay attention though and know what size shoes you wear." When he released me I turned and took the sweaters out of the bag.

Pulling his shirt off over his head he tried them on. They were a perfect fit and he made them look awesome stretched over his hard chest and shoulders.

He looked like a kid in a candy store the way he smiled as he modeled them for me.

"I know you need to get some sleep tonight, but I'd still like you to stay over if you will." He said pulling me close again.

I nuzzled my head into his chest, enjoying the warmth of his arms. "Of course I'll stay with you." The truth was I had come to hate going to bed alone and waking up with the spot next to me empty.

SEVENTEEN

The next month passed in a blur. With the holiday season upon us there were parties planned for the next two months. The three big ones were the company Halloween, Christmas and New Year's parties.

In between there was the regular hustle of Thanksgiving and Christmas dinners with family. After getting my budget worked out I had decided I would try to go home for Thanksgiving. I missed my sisters.

Adam and I had discussed our plans and agreed that he would come home with me to meet my family at Thanksgiving and I would spend Christmas with him and his family. It seemed the logical thing to do since I really couldn't afford two trips so close together. Plus I didn't have a lot of vacation time either.

I called my mom and talked to her for a long time about Adam and to let her know we would be coming in for Thanksgiving. She was excited that I was coming home for at least one holiday and looking forward to meeting my '*new man*' as she put it.

Then right before I hung up she told me that Joe had stopped by. She said he was looking pretty miserable but just wanted to know if I was doing okay. She hadn't told him much, not really knowing what to say. I hoped that I didn't have to see him when I visited.

Davy and Gloria had come back from their honeymoon with a ton of pictures and we spent one afternoon pouring over them. Gloria seemed to have blossomed overnight and now boasted a baby bump the size of half a basketball.

Davy joked that it was his bouncing baby boy. Gloria rolled her eyes saying "I wouldn't be too sure about that."

Amy spent nearly every weekend away with Paul but we made a point to eat lunch together at least a couple times a week.

Ned still lurked around corners, listening in on conversations and sulking. I didn't want to talk to him, but at the same time I really wanted to know what was eating at him. There was definitely something going on with him when it came to Adam.

The annual company Halloween party was held the Saturday before the actual holiday since it fell midweek this year. The entire first and second floors of the Jameson building were decorated with spider web and eerie lighting just for the occasion. Waiters walked around with trays of h'orderves and a bar had been set up for drinks.

Adam and I had gone all out on our costumes, dressing up as Batman and Catwoman. I had wanted to be Wonder Woman but my boobs were too small for the costume. It was probably just as well since it turned out freezing that night. The Catwoman suit was warm.

Shortly after we arrived Amy and Paul came in dressed as Wonder Woman and Superman. I noticed she had no problem filling out the top and I was really glad I had decided on another costume. Ned came in a little later dressed as a Nerd. At least I think he was dressed up. Maybe he was just being himself.

All in all I counted about ten "Barbies" all varying versions, and a couple of Ken's. Every other person was a vampire or a witch and a couple of people were dressed as Jason with a hockey mask and knife.

247

There were some flappers, some mummies, one sumo wrestler, one Jessica Rabbit, and even a couple of Harry Potters. Adam and I were the only Batman and Catwoman.

The party went well for the first few hours. The food was good and the drinks were good, but flowing a little too freely. After a while it became apparent how much alcohol had been consumed.

People were getting louder and bolder. Inhibitions were dropping like flies. One of the flappers was attempting the Charleston on top of a table and not doing too good.

A few of the men had started calling "Here kitty kitty," every time I got close to them. I noticed that Adam was staying close by, his jaw clenching with every jab.

Finally he whispered "Let's get out of here before the real fun starts."

"Alright," I agreed, but I needed to use the restroom first.

Coming out of the ladies room I was accosted by a very angry, very drunk Ned.

"I guess you two think you are so cute traipsing around here in your little costumes. You think you're really a couple."

I didn't want to get into an argument with an inebriated idiot so I tried to walk around him. That apparently only made him angrier. Grabbing me by the arm he swung me around to face him.

"Don't think you can just walk away from me while I'm talking to you." He slurred, spraying spittle everywhere.

"What the hell is wrong with you Ned?" I demanded, jerking my arm free. "Something has been eating at you for weeks now and I'd like to know what it is."

"What's wrong with me? What's wrong with ME?" He nearly shouted. "Why don't you ask what is wrong with Adam. Why don't you ask him about Carrie and what he did to her?"

I moved back away from him. "I don't know anyone named Carrie." I spouted back angrily. I didn't know what he was talking about and suddenly I felt ill. *Who is Carrie?*

As if reading my thoughts, Ned started up again. "Carrie was my girl. She was with me until Adam came on the scene and stole her away from me.

Then what did he do? He broke her heart. Dropped her like a hot potato and don't you think for one minute that he won't ditch you too when he gets tired of you."

He was walking forward, yelling at me and I was steadily moving back trying to get away from him.

Then suddenly Batman appeared out of nowhere grabbing Ned by the front of the shirt. With one hand he lifted him into the air, shoving him up against the wall, holding him there. His jaw muscles were working overtime as he fought the urge to body slam Ned into the floor.

Ned was so drunk he had no idea what was happening. His eyes almost bulged out of his head as he stared down at the Dark Knight; his hands up against the wall in surrender.

"Don't hurt me." He squeaked.

I thought for a minute he might wet his pants. And then I saw it. That wicked little grin that Adam gets sometimes slowly crept across his mouth. When he opened his mouth to speak it was no longer Adam Knight but the voice of Batman, perfectly imitated.

"You just made a serious mistake." He said in that low, husky whisper.

Ned looked like he might cry. "I'm sorry, I won't do it again. Please don't hurt me."

Adam slowly let Ned slide down the wall until he was resting on his feet again.

"Stay away from my woman or next time you won't get off so easy." He said still using his Batman voice.

Ned scurried off back to the party. I couldn't believe what had just happened. I wanted to find out about Carrie, but right now that just wasn't important. What was important – I would never think about Batman the same again - Ever.

"Wow, talk about the Dark Knight Rises!" I said taking Adam's hand as we walked out the door together.

Adam growled in my ear. "He's been rising since you put on that outfit tonight."

Adam opened the car door for me then went around to the other side. Climbing into the driver's seat he settled behind the wheel.

"What the hell was that all about in there anyway? What was that idiot yelling about?"

I turned in my seat so that I could see Adam's face, or at least the part that wasn't covered by his mask. "He's angry at you." I stated.

"At me? What for," he asked, apparently having no idea.

"Who is Carrie?" I asked, still watching to gauge his reaction.

Adam thought for a moment. "The only Carrie I know is a girl I dated a while back. What does she have to do with anything?"

"According to Ned she was his girl and you stole her from him."

Adam looked positively shocked. "What the hell?"

"He claims that you stole her from him then dumped her and broke her heart."

Adam rubbed a hand over his face, seemingly in deep thought. "I guess the first time I met her maybe she was with him. It was at a company function, but I didn't pursue her."

"It was several weeks later. I was out having a drink. She recognized me from the party and came over and we started talking."

Reaching over he took my hand in his, glancing at me momentarily. "I asked her out and she said yes. If she was with Ned she never mentioned it, and if I broke her heart I truly had no idea. We only went on maybe three dates over a couple of months."

"I just stopped calling her because I knew she wasn't the one. I was getting tired of dating just anyone. As far as I knew she was seeing other people too."

He glanced over at me again. "You believe me don't you?"

"Yes, of course I believe you Adam. Why would you think different?"

"I just don't want anything to mess us up; especially someone that I never even gave a second thought about. And I don't want you thinking I would leave you and break your heart."

I squeezed his hand a little tighter. I felt bad for even entertaining the idea. It seemed that Ned just had a skewed perception of things.

But regardless broken hearts were just part of life. We've all had one at one time or another. I knew Adam would never intentionally hurt anyone, and I knew he loved me.

EIGHTEEN

The days grew progressively colder as we moved through November. Thanksgiving was just a week away. Airline tickets had been purchased and rental cars reserved for my trip home. I couldn't wait.

Monday, the night before our flight out, I lie in bed next to Adam. He had been pretty quiet all evening and now stared up at the ceiling, his fingers trailing softly up and down my arm. I rolled over on my side, supporting my head on one hand.

"Is everything okay?" I asked thinking maybe he was nervous about meeting my family.

He rolled onto his side facing me, continuing to rub his hand up and down my arm.

"I've just been thinking of something." He said then paused. His hand stopped its track down my arm. "The lease on my apartment will be up in January. I'll have to renew it…unless…I move somewhere else."

My heart sank in my chest. Where else would he go? How far away? I knew there was the possibility of him transferring if he got the position Larry had spoken to him about but I had pushed that thought from the forefront of my mind. Now it suddenly came rushing back with a vengeance.

"Where would you want to move to?" The thought of him being far away from me seemed to be suffocating me. I barely got the words out of my mouth.

"I was thinking…maybe…if you're not opposed, I could move in with you. We practically live together anyway."

Not realizing I'd been holding my breath, I suddenly released it, able to breathe once again.

Quickly he added, "If it's too soon for you I'll understand."

I leaned into his chest, nuzzling my nose against his skin. "No, it's okay. I think it's a good idea. I was just afraid you were going to move away."

"Baby if I go anywhere you can be damn sure I'm taking you with me."

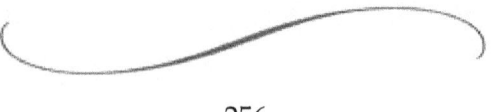

The plane touched down at Bergstrom International Airport in Austin. I had told Adam to pack for warmer weather and throw in a jacket and cool weather wear just in case. The weather forecast was calling for a wet, but not necessarily cold Thanksgiving Day.

The weather was the one thing about Austin that I didn't miss; sweltering hot in the summer with a few cold days in the winter and only a hint of spring or fall. I was keeping my fingers crossed that the temperature would drop for Thanksgiving. It was so un-holiday like when it was still warm outside.

Picking up our rental car I drove us to my parent's house where we would be staying for the next three days. Two of my sisters still lived with my parents so it was sure to be one huge slumber party. Adam and I would stay in my old room.

The family home was actually outside of Austin in a little town called Dripping Springs. There nestled among the rolling hills, rock and prickly pear cactus was the two-story, frame house I'd grown up in.

It wasn't really all that bad. In fact there were a lot of beautiful rock formations and natural springs that were truly breathtaking to see. There just wasn't much to do around town except sit around and drink the local vodka when you were bored. It was damn good vodka though.

When I pulled into the drive I was surprised to see that Dad had finally built the tool shed he'd always wanted and extended the parking area. With all my sister's cars in the drive they needed the extra space.

I had three younger sisters and one older brother. My brother Daniel was Adam's age and had moved out when he was eighteen. I think he must have been going crazy with all of us girls around.

He had moved to the Houston area for a better job and more excitement, as he had put it. He would be coming in this evening, driving up. From what mom had said he was bringing a girl with him.

My brother had dated a lot of girls but he'd never brought one home for the holidays before. I wondered if he was getting serious about this one.

Janie was twenty-four and still living at home with my parents. My dad referred to her as the *level-headed* one. She was still in school and that was her sole focus, absolutely refusing to date while she worked on her degree.

Of all us girls I considered her the over-achiever. Mediocre was never good enough for her. It had to be perfect but sometimes I felt that she was missing out on life in her pursuit of perfection. Regardless she managed to keep her sense of humor.

Lana was twenty-two and living on her own. She had chosen not to go to college, taking a job in Austin right out of high school. She had started out in sales and was now managing the small clothing store.

As far as I could tell she was doing pretty well, working a lot and making sure bills were paid on time, but she also took time for herself. She'd had a couple of boyfriends in the last two years but nothing she seemed to take too seriously.

My baby sister, Jules was almost nineteen and would graduate in June. She had plans to go to college then med school, but like Janie and myself, would have to get student loans to do so. My parents would help as much as they could, but what they could contribute wouldn't go very far towards a med-school tuition. With any luck Jules might get a scholarship she'd applied for. She was at the top of her class.

Her real name was Julie but we called her Jules and sometimes Joules. The latter was a nickname Daniel had given her when she was five, when she had decided to stick a hairpin into an electrical outlet.

Fortunately it had not killed her but it did seem to make her hair frizzy for a while. She never tried it again. It was years before I learned what joules even were. I had just called her that because Daniel did. However the name stuck.

I looked at Adam. "Are you ready for this?"

He smiled back at me. "Ready as I'll ever be."

We grabbed our suitcases out of the trunk and made our way to the front door. Just as we stepped onto the porch the front door was jerked open by Janie. Her eyes went from Adam to me then back to Adam.

"Damn Drew, where did you find him?" She asked me, grinning at Adam.

"Doesn't matter," I replied. "He was the last one so you're out of luck." Then looking at Adam, who was now grinning from ear to ear, I said "You'll have to excuse my sisters. Sometimes they forget how to make someone feel welcome."

"Well of course he's welcome." Janie countered. "We haven't had something this pretty to look at in ages." She smiled at Adam again. "Y'all come in. I'm Janie by the way."

Adam stepped inside and held out his hand to her. "Adam Knight." He said, enjoying her flirtatious banter.

Janie looked at his hand then laughed. "Sorry we don't shake hands with family." She said, pulling him down in a hug. Janie was blessed with the big hips and breasts but she was a clean five inches shorter than me. In fact, at five foot-ten inches, I was taller than everyone except Daniel.

Mom appeared around the corner wiping her hands on a dishtowel. She had been baking, evidenced by the flour on her apron and the aromas of pies and breads wafting through the house.

"Oh you've made it in." She said coming toward us. She hugged me, kissing my cheek. "Drew honey, have you lost more weight?" She asked eyeing me up and down. "I don't remember you being that thin before."

"No mamma, I haven't lost any more weight." I said setting my suitcase down.

She turned to Adam. "You must be Adam." She said smiling, reaching up to hug him.

"Yes ma'am." Adam replied.

"I'm so happy to finally meet you. I'm Drew's mom. Most people call me Ellen." Mom said, then turning back to me. "Drew you two can put your stuff away in your old room."

"There's food in the kitchen if you kids are hungry. I'm baking now but you know where everything is. Just help yourselves. Daniel and Lana should be along sometime today." She turned, heading back into the kitchen.

I led the way upstairs to my old room. Once inside I shut the door. "I hope my family is not overwhelming you."

"Not at all, they kind of remind me of my own family. I'm glad you invited me along."

"Are you hungry?" I asked feeling my stomach growl as I asked him.

"Actually I'm starving." He said pulling me against him.

I nuzzled against him accepting the kisses he was liberally bestowing on my face.

"Let's go to the kitchen and I'll find us something to eat."

We ran into Janie in the hall. "Where are you two headed?" She asked.

"Kitchen," I replied. "We're starving.

"Me too, I'll come with. Mom made sourdough and there's roast beef in the fridge."

"A roast beef sandwich sounds awesome right now." Adam said.

Reaching the refrigerator I took out stuff for sandwiches then dug around until I found a jar of horseradish. Adam sat at the island looking at the assortment of pies. There were at least a dozen; all different kinds.

"Mom always cooks for an army." I explained.

"That's a lot of pie." Adam said, his mouth starting to water.

Mom came over to the island. "What kinds of pie do you like Adam?" She asked.

"I like just about everything."

"Then which would you prefer?"

"Umm, that chocolate cream looks good." Mom turned back to her baking. She was stirring something on the stove, maybe more pudding.

"Drew, cut him a piece of that chocolate pie." She continued, not looking at us. "You know Adam, Drew knows how to make all these pies too."

I rolled my eyes as I handed him a slice. "I believe it." He said. "She is a great cook."

I sliced up some sourdough then Janie, Adam and I sat and ate roast beef sandwiches and pie.

"Where's Jules?" I asked, realizing I'd not seen her or dad yet.

"She's got a part-time job and offered to work for one of her friends. She should be in later. Your dad had to work today too but he's off the rest of the week." Mom said.

"Do you need any help in the kitchen?"

"I'm just about done with the baking for now. You and Adam go relax a while. You can help me with breakfast in the morning."

I was tired. It had been a long day on the plane and an hour drive out to the house. I knew Adam was tired too so I suggested a nap before my dad got home.

Adam was more than willing to rest up as well. Climbing into my old bed I snuggled against his back and was asleep as soon as my head hit the pillow.

I woke up hearing Daniel's voice in the hallway. It was six p.m. I was still tired but I knew I wouldn't sleep tonight if I didn't get up. Adam stirred next to me, his eyes opening sleepily.

"What time is it?" He asked, stretching his arms overhead.

"Six." I told him, kissing him on the nose. "Daniel is here. Let's go see him."

Without warning he grabbed me around the waist and rolled over on top of me, pinning me to the bed. A sleepy smile touched his eyes as he held me there.

"I think I should take advantage of you now before I meet your brother. He might want to beat me up." He said as he started to nibble on my lower lip.

"He might," I laughed, "but the girls have him outnumbered and we won't let him. Besides, he's probably worried about me beating up his girlfriend!"

"Oh, I see Ducky is back. Should I prepare a swimming pool full of mud for the fight?"

"Don't push your luck." I said laughing.

"Okay," he said giving me one last kiss. "Let's go meet your brother."

We went down into the main living area where everyone was gathering. Dad and Jules had made it in from work and Lana was dragging her suitcase through the front door.

Daniel stood as we entered the room. He was bigger than I remembered or maybe he had packed on a few pounds. I hadn't seen him in over a year. It was all muscle though. He looked great.

"Come here squirt." He called to me, his arms outstretched.

I walked right into them, wrapping my arms around his waist. It was so good to see him again. I pulled back from him and craned my neck up to see him. Damn, I didn't remember him being this tall either.

"What did you do?" I asked. "Grow some more since the last time I saw you?"

"Naw, you're just wearing flats is all. But you are definitely skinnier than the last time I saw you. You're not on one of those starvation diets are you?"

I just laughed. "Nope, I like to eat way too much. I just lost some weight this summer and haven't gained it back."

He cut his eyes at me. "It was that fucker Joe wasn't it? I warned you he'd break your heart."

Lana ducked under Daniel's arm dragging her suitcase behind her. She suddenly seemed a little pale as she jerked the suitcase onto the landing and hurried up the stairs. Her behavior struck me as odd, but I quickly put it out of my mind.

I nodded. "Yes you did. But that is all done with now." I motioned for Adam to join me. "Daniel I want you to meet Adam. Adam this is my brother Daniel."

The look that Daniel gave Adam was almost as bad as the one Adam had given Lucy's boyfriend. However, if it fazed him he didn't let on. He simply extended his hand to Daniel and maintained eye contact.

Daniel was physically larger than Adam but it was clear that Adam was not the least intimidated by that fact. I was already proud of him, but in that moment the pride swelled so big in my chest it threatened to choke me.

267

"I won't break her heart." He stated matter of fact to Daniel, and suddenly the tension broke and Daniel grabbed his hand and slapped him on the back. The closest I've ever seen him come to hugging another guy.

We all got to meet Corinne. She was very pretty and petite and possibly overwhelmed by our family. She was quiet and seemed a bit shy so I made a point of including her in our conversation.

Joules was non-stop talk, her mouth moving faster than a New Yorker's, telling us all about school and her job and her plan's for college. She barely took a breath between sentences and I wondered if she'd taken a class to talk that fast.

Lana returned from upstairs and greeted everyone then opened a bottle of wine, pouring us each some.

My dad came around to meet Adam and Corinne then took off his work boots and fell into his recliner. Eating a sandwich mom brought him he pushed back in the chair and was soon snoring.

Adam and Daniel sat animatedly talking about football. I sat next to Janie who seemed to be pre-occupied with a constant stream of texts on her phone. Occasionally she would look up at me and Adam and I thought I heard her sigh a time or two.

"Okay, spill it." I demanded quietly where only she could hear.

She looked startled at my demand.

"Tell me about him. You know you can't hide anything from me. I haven't seen you look like this since Jonah didn't ask you to prom. So what is his name?"

She hesitated for just a minute then smiled. "His name is Michael, but I'm not dating him."

I rolled my eyes at her, "But?"

"But I really do like him and we talk all the time and now he's driving me crazy wanting to see me over the holidays."

"So why not invite him for dinner Thursday?"

She shrugged her shoulders.

"Don't you want to see him too? Or are you afraid for him to meet the family."

Janie laughed. "No he might as well get broke in good from the beginning, but I don't want to lose focus on my school either."

I sighed. I couldn't believe my ears. "Janie, you only have one more semester before you're done. It's not likely you, of all people, will lose your focus.

You are trying too hard to be perfect at the expense of your own feelings. There is nothing wrong with spending a day with him or a night for that matter."

She sighed again. "I don't know. I'll think about it."

Mom called her into the kitchen and Janie got up, leaving her phone on the end table.

Lana came over and sat next to me. "What was that all about?" She asked, talking about our whispered conversation.

"Janie likes someone." Just then her phone vibrated and I couldn't resist temptation. Picking it up I read the screen. It was from Michael.

"Is that him?" Lana asked.

I smiled. "Yes."

Jules suddenly appeared wanting in on the secret. I held up the screen for everyone to read.

"Let's invite him out." I said to the others. "We won't tell Janie and we'll make him keep it a surprise."

"Okay." They both said at the same time. "Let's do it."

Quickly I flipped through her phone, found Michael's number and programmed it into my phone, replacing Janie's phone on the end table.

The three of us gathered close together and I snapped our picture then sent it with a text to Michael. I told him who we were and invited him to come spend the holiday with us, letting him know that Janie was here with us, but not to tell her.

The reply was instantaneous.

Michael: → *Yes, when can I come?*

Drew: → *Now if you want. Let me know so we can be expecting you*

Michael: → *I can leave within the hour. Can you text me the address?*

Quickly I sent him the address. Lana and Jules were still hovering over my shoulder whispering and giggling. I knew if Janie saw us all hovering she'd know something was up.

"Better scatter now." I said. "I'll let y'all know when he leaves."

Forty-five minutes later he texted me to say he was leaving and should be here in just over an hour.

I knew Janie might pretend to hate me for this but it would be short lived. I was her sister. She wasn't allowed to hate me for long.

Dad was still asleep in the recliner so I woke him up and sent him to bed. Adam and Daniel were still talking sports so I left them to it. Corinne seemed to be content to stay next Daniel. Occasionally he would reach over and pull her closer.

Janie came back and sat down next to me again. "Mom said to tell you she's calling it a night."

Picking up her phone she glanced at the screen then answered her last text. I noticed that she would pick up her phone every few minutes checking to see if there was a new message. There was nothing.

As the hour passed she was getting anxious. Michael had not texted her back. Of course I knew he wouldn't but this was driving her crazy.

She really had it bad for this guy and seemed to be staring at her phone a lot, willing it to vibrate with a message from him. Being the decent person I am, raised with good moral standards and all, I decided to make her sweat.

"What's wrong Janie? He's not texting back?"

"No. I guess maybe he's busy."

"Did you invite him to dinner?"

"No. Maybe if he'd text back I would."

"Oh, well he doesn't have any other friends does he? Maybe someone else invited him for dinner and he gave up on you."

She shot me a dirty look. I was getting to her.

"Maybe he just went to bed," she said. "It is kind of late."

Lana and Jules picked up on the conversation and came over. When it came to acting we were pretty damn good at it, especially when it was tied to a practical joke.

"What's wrong Janie?" Lana asked. "You look like you might be sick."

"Nothing is wrong with me." Janie mumbled.

Lana looked at the phone in her lap. "Who's Michael?" She asked, biting back a grin.

"Just a friend," Janie replied.

"Oh, he's not texting you back huh?" Lana said acting concerned.

"Okay y'all, let her alone." I told them. "She doesn't care whether or not some dumb guy texts her back."

"He's not dumb!" Janie blurted out at me. I was pushing her buttons now but I knew I should stop before she got mad. Michael should be arriving any time now. Janie looked to be on the verge of tears.

"I'm going to bed." She abruptly announced. I was suddenly frantic trying to think of some way to keep her downstairs when the doorbell rang.

"Well, can you answer the door on your way up?"

Janie huffed and rolled her eyes. Getting up she walked to the door, unaware of the audience that was following at a distance. Lana readied the camera in her phone.

I'll never forget the look on Janie's face when she opened the door to find Michael standing there. She stood staring for a minute before she fell into his arms crying. He pulled her close, kissing her like he was starving and she was his last meal. She didn't resist.

Adam came up behind me, wrapping his arms around my shoulders. "Looks like he has the right idea," He whispered in my ear.

I looked up to find everyone had come out of the living room to see what we were up to. Corinne stood next to Daniel smiling at Janie and Michael. Daniel was gawking, shaking his head in disbelief.

"There's only one of me. How am I supposed to keep an eye on the boyfriends of two sisters at the same time?"

We wound up staying up late into the night playing board games and eating popcorn and making margaritas. Janie seemed content that Michael was with her, at least after she promised us girls payback for our little joke. Michael was overjoyed to be spending time with her.

Lana opened another bottle of wine and came to sit with me. I'd heard that she had yet another young man in her life and wondered if we'd get to meet this one.

"Did you invite your new guy friend out this year?" I asked fishing for information.

She shrugged. "I did, but I don't think he is going to show up," she said gulping down her glass of wine.

She seemed a little out of sorts about it so I didn't push her for more information. She would tell me about it when she was ready to.

NINETEEN

I'm not sure where the weather man got his information from but he was dead wrong. On Wednesday evening, after a beautiful day of playing flag football, the wind started blowing and the temperature plummeted. It was freezing cold and drizzling rain.

We brought in a ton of firewood and started a huge fire in the fireplace. Mom made hot chocolate and hot spiced cider and we all sat around sipping our mugs, telling stories of when we were kids.

I made a pumpkin roll to go with our drinks, as if we didn't have enough to eat already. Lana found a bottle of coconut rum somewhere and we spiked our hot chocolate with it.

With the alcohol and the warmth of the fire I was soon yawning, ready for bed. Adam kissed my cheek.

"Let's go get a shower and get some sleep." I nodded, rising from my chair, allowing him to lead me off.

After our shower I snuggled against him in the bed. It was still pretty cool in the room and getting into bed was like crawling into an ice box. The rain was now coming down in sheets, being driven into the walls and windows of the house by a fierce wind.

Outside the night was black as pitch. Looking from my bedroom window I was unable to see anything except when, for a brief moment lightning split the sky, illuminating the ominous clouds that filled it. Claps of thunder seemed to roll on endlessly.

The house shuddered violently under the icy wind, groaning and creaking with each brutal gust. Rolling up a towel I placed it against my window to block the cold air from seeping through.

This was perfect weather for being in bed. I wiggled even closer against Adam sliding my hands under his shirt, feeling the warmth of his skin. I needed him.

He pulled me closer, his mouth finding mine, tenderly devouring me. My arousal flared immediately. He needed me too.

"We probably shouldn't be doing this in your parent's house." He whispered mischievously. "If your brother finds out he might beat me up."

I giggled. "I think the wind and rain are so loud we could do whatever we wanted to and no-one would ever even hear us."

The good thing was my parents had converted the formal living room into a downstairs master bedroom about a year ago. My dad said his old bones couldn't stand climbing the stairs anymore.

Their room was on the other side of the house and none of the upstairs rooms were above it. That way they wouldn't be bothered by us kids beating around while they were trying to sleep. I had a feeling there was going to be a lot of beating around up here tonight.

"Is your door locked?"

"Yes I locked it." Then, remembering Janie's threat of a payback I got up and checked it, putting some pillows at the base of the door to block any noise. *It would be just like Janie to sneak in with a camera...*

By morning the wind and rain had moved through leaving a dry, cold, sunny day in its wake. It was going to be a perfect Thanksgiving Day. Mom was already up in the kitchen when I came down and started fixing breakfast for everyone.

Slowly everyone trickled in to the kitchen as the smell of sausage, eggs and coffee reached their noses. Jules was the last one to drag herself to the breakfast table. She looked as though she'd had a rough night, dark circles under her eyes. Everyone else seemed to be rested and happy

"What's wrong with you this morning?" Dad asked noticing her sour expression.

"I didn't get much sleep." She said grumpily. "I think we have another rat."

Mom sighed. "I sure hope not."

"What makes you think that?" Dad asked.

"Because something kept waking me up scraping on the walls last night."

"Are you sure it wasn't the wind honey?" Mom asked. "It was pretty wild last night."

"No it was the inside walls; first the one by my head then the one on the other end of the room. And I heard some squeaking too."

I thought of how the rooms were positioned upstairs and almost laughed. Julie's room was between Daniel's old one and Janie's. More than likely she was hearing the other beds scraping up against the wall and squeaky bed frames.

I looked at Daniel then at Janie. The latter cut her eyes at me and dared me to say anything. Daniel looked unaffected but poor Corinne was a new shade of red.

"I don't think you have rats Dad." I said, "more like rabbits."

Adam suddenly winced as if in pain. Janie's eyes widened in alarm, "Oh my god, I'm so sorry. I meant to kick Drew."

"What the hell are you kicking your sister's boyfriend for?" Dad wanted to know. Michael and Lana were sniggering and Corinne was blushing even more. Jules seemed oblivious to everything.

Dad rolled his eyes. "Can we just eat our breakfast now please and we'll worry about the rats later."

The rest of the day was pleasant with friends stopping by here and there. The pies that mom had made earlier in the week were all but gone. I rubbed my belly. I think I'd gained about five pounds in the last two days.

Lana left that evening, heading back to Austin. She told everyone she had to open the shop early for Black-Friday sales. I think she wanted to get back to her mystery man. She just seemed too eager to leave. Adam and I would be flying back tomorrow at noon. Daniel and Corinne were leaving in the morning.

We were up early again the next morning, packed and ready to go. After a big breakfast and saying our goodbyes, we headed to the airport. Just before boarding the plane I got a text from Lana.

Joe came into the shop today. Seems to be doing good. Asked about you... wanted to know how you're doing. Told him you're happy - doing good – Adam good for you. Hope you're ok with that.

I didn't reply. I hoped Joe was moving on. Despite how bad he'd hurt me I still cared for him. He had really done me a huge favor. I never would have met Adam if Joe hadn't left me. I knew Adam was the best thing that had ever happened to me.

Another month was flying by as we moved through December. It was cold but hadn't reached freezing temperatures yet. It was just so wet and nasty...and gray outside.

Despite the gloom of the weather the atmosphere remained cheerful. With Christmas just days away we had a lot to do. Our company party was this weekend then Adam and I would drive to Everett to spend Christmas Day with his family. I was more than a little nervous about meeting his family.

Things were changing fast. Adam had given notice to the leasing office that he would be moving after the first of the year and would not be renewing his lease. Also he was waiting to hear from Larry about the Bainbridge office opening. Nothing more had been said since their meeting two months ago.

One of the elevators was out of order so it was taking longer than normal to call a car. The repair man had been around all week working on it. It seemed like I saw him on every floor. His name was Denny but because the company logo was written across his back I had started referring to him as Otis.

He was always polite when I saw him and I'd started talking to him while he worked and I waited for the car. He had been working for the company repairing elevators for twenty-five years. Normally it didn't take him this long to fix one, but he'd had to wait on parts. I hoped it was fixed by next week.

Saturday morning we got up early and went to the gym. After that we went to see Davy and Gloria. I had put together a basket for them for Christmas. Actually it was for the baby and a little something for them but I knew Gloria would love it.

She had chosen her colors for the nursery so I went and found toys and accessories that would match. I kept it gender neutral since they had opted not to find out the baby's sex. Davy still contended that it was a boy, but Gloria said she felt like it was a girl.

I wrapped the basket up in colored cellophane and put a huge bow at the top. Adam carried it in. It must have weighed thirty pounds with all the stuff in it.

Gloria was thrilled to see us, chattering the whole way as she waddled to meet us. She was bigger every time I saw her and I wondered if maybe there weren't two babies in that belly of hers.

She stuck out so far she could balance a plate on top of her belly and told me she had to when she ate because she could no longer sit up straight. The baby kicked too much when she did.

I bent over rubbing and talking to her belly. "Hello in there. This is your aunt Drew." I got an immediate kick.

"She must have heard you." Gloria said.

"You mean He." Davy countered.

"Whatevah," Gloria said, waving her hand dismissively. "You guys come on in. Davy put the gift under the tree."

"What – you mean you're gonna make me wait to open it?" He said taking the basket from Adam.

Gloria rolled her eyes. "If you open it now you won't have anything to open on Christmas day." She said tartly. "You have been very naughty this year. Santa doesn't bring bad boys presents."

"Well I got something last year and I wasn't any badder this year."

"Yes you were."

"How so?"

"You knocked me up. That's how so!" Gloria said matter of fact.

Davy grinned. "Guess I can't deny that one." He said pulling Gloria close, kissing her. Then swatting her on the butt said "And I'd do it again too."

"Yeah, Yeah, We'll see how this one goes first."

Unlike the Halloween party that had been held in the Jameson building, the Christmas party was held at the Fairmont Olympic Hotel in one of the large conference rooms.

It had been set up with a full buffet in a connected side room, an open bar, and a dance floor in the main room. Surrounding the dance floor were dozens of large round tables, each seating ten people.

The room was decorated in festive red, green and gold and an enormous Christmas tree stood at one end. Each table had a red tablecloth and a crystal centerpiece filled with greenery and red and gold ornaments.

There were no guidelines for dress, just whatever you wanted to wear. Some people went all out wearing tuxedos and ball gowns while others wore casual slacks and skirts.

Adam and I dressed somewhere in between. I wore an ankle length, emerald green dress made of satin embellished with beads. It was sleeveless, princess seamed with a sweetheart neckline and a low-cut back. Adam wore his black suit with a light green shirt and emerald green tie.

Paul had come down to be Amy's date for the occasion and they sat with us and a few others from our floor. Ned was there with a date and he seemed to be enjoying himself for once. I hoped we didn't have a repeat of our Halloween party. He hadn't said much to me since that night.

After dinner Adam led me out to the dance floor where we danced through a couple of songs. I was surprised when Larry cut in on one of the dances. He was quite a good dancer, leading me easily through the moves.

"You know," he started, "you quite remind me of my granddaughter. You both are tall and slender and have long brown hair."

"I didn't know that." I replied.

"Yes, I miss her something terrible. She went off to London and fell in love with a British young man. Going to marry him and live there. I'm planning a trip to visit her soon."

"That's very nice. You will have a good reason to go to Europe often."

"Yes." He was thoughtful for a few moments. "I wasn't aware that you and Adam were seeing each other. I don't get out of my office enough. Is it serious?"

I was surprised that he was asking me about my relationship with Adam but didn't feel threatened by the question. He seemed genuinely interested. Adam and I had never tried to keep anything hidden from work so I felt it was okay to answer honestly.

"Well, we love each other if that's what you mean by serious. We're planning to move in together soon."

Larry looked thoughtful. The song was ending and he bowed his head, kissing the back of my hand. "Thank you for the dance. It was lovely. And thank you for being honest to a nosy old man."

I smiled at him. "You're welcome Mr. Jameson."

"Please, just call me Larry." Then he left the floor as Adam returned to claim me.

"That was a nice dance." I said to Adam when he returned.

"Well don't get too use to dancing with other men. He's probably the only one I'll ever give you up to; except your dad."

I leaned into him. I liked it when he was possessive of me.

"Have I told you how beautiful you look tonight?" He asked me, pulling me closer against him.

"No. Tell me." I whispered in his ear.

"You are the most beautiful woman I have ever seen. And I will always love you."

I leaned back to look into his eyes. "And I will never stop loving you."

The dance ended and we left the dance floor, returning to our table. Adam went to the bar and came back a few minutes later with drinks. We sat for a while talking to Amy and Paul as the dessert trays were being brought around.

"Who is the girl Ned is with?" I whispered to Amy when I had a chance.

"Her name is Tabitha. She is the daughter of Louis Brown. I'm not exactly sure what his title is but his office is on the eighth floor with Larry's so he must me important."

I nodded. "I was just curious."

"Yea me too, I had to ask Melissa and she had asked Lee Ann. I guess we were all curious."

We left the party just before midnight. I had a lot to do tomorrow. Monday we were going to

Everett. His parents only lived about thirty-five miles away but we were going to stay the night Christmas Eve and spend Christmas Day with them.

I had been worried about gifts for everyone. Since I didn't know anyone but Lucy I had no clue what they might like. Adam assured me that gifts weren't necessary, but also the one's he'd gotten would be from both of us. I opted to bring a large edible fruit basket anyway.

The gift I'd gotten for Adam wasn't something he could open in front of his family. I'd had an album of boudoir photos put together for him. Getting it made had been near impossible. It required that I sneak away from work without Adam finding out I was gone. I had to meet the photographer at a local hotel.

Randy had known I had an appointment so leaving work wasn't the problem. Amy had kept her eyes and ears open, ready to make something up should Adam show up looking for me.

The photo shoot had cost me a small fortune but it was worth it. The album turned out great, and the pictures made me look like a model. Cindy, the photographer, was awesome at her job. She had re-touched the photos to erase every imperfection.

Buying a gift for Adam that he could open in front of his family had been a challenge. I honestly didn't know what he'd want. He didn't wear jewelry and I didn't want to buy him a sweater for Christmas. I called Davy for a little help in this department.

"Sweetheart I have just the ticket for you." He said enthusiastically. "Tickets actually, I just got hooked up with someone who has four super bowl 2013 tickets in New Orleans that they have to sell. I would love to go but I don't think G- will be able to fly then. I could pick up a couple for you though. They're good seats and he's selling them at a good price."

I jumped on the deal when Davy told me how much. Adam loved sports and I knew he would enjoy going to the super bowl no matter who was playing. This would be the perfect gift. He would never buy this for himself.

Monday afternoon, with everything loaded into Adam's car, we drove up to Everett. The sky had cleared for a while and the sun was out. It was a gorgeous day.

I tried to remember everything Adam had told me about his family. His mother was Rebecca and his dad was Jim. They were several years older than my parents. Adam was the third of five children.

His oldest brother, Jerry, was almost eight years older than him. Anne, his older sister was four years older. After Adam, his brother Tom was twenty-five and Lucy twenty-four. I had already forgotten who was married, divorced, etc. I did know that Jared would be coming with Lucy.

Then there were the nieces and nephews. Adam spoke about them often but I had a hard time keeping up with who was whose. There were only five of them.

The oldest belonged to Jerry. His name was Nathan and he would not be here this year. He was overseas in Pakistan. Everyone was just hoping for his safe return.

When we pulled into the drive I was shocked. Adam had said he grew up in a big house but I had no idea it was this big. You could easily fit two of my parent's house into it; maybe three.

It was an older, two-story home, all red brick with a huge front porch that stuck out from the face of the entirely square home. The balcony above the porch provided shade and protection below. It was also covered making the structure two tiers high.

It was not esthetically pleasing, but plain and bulky, having none of the graceful lines newer homes boasted. The yard however was neatly trimmed and landscaped adding beauty to the front of the home.

"This is where you grew up?" I asked, suddenly feeling out of place. This was way out of my league.

Adam squeezed my hand. "This is the place. I know it's an imposing old house but don't let it intimidate you. It's just a house."

He came around and opened my door for me. Pulling me to my feet and into his arms he kissed me.

"You have no idea how happy I am that you're here with me." He said kissing me again. "Thank you for coming."

"There's no-where I'd rather be than with you, wherever that is." I said. And I really meant it.

Entering the house I realized immediately that even though it was old, it had been remodeled and modernized inside. It was incredibly spacious with an open floor plan. From where I was standing near the front door I could see a massive, two-sided fireplace dividing the living room from a formal sitting area.

Adam's parents were both very nice and I liked them at once. His mother was slender and well dressed. Her hair almost completely gray, hung thick and straight down to her shoulders in a blunt cut. She had the same deep blue eyes as Adam.

His dad also had gray hair cut short and was wearing jeans and a polo shirt. His arms were tanned a deep brown making his skin appear almost leathery. I assumed he spent many hours on the water.

Rebecca greeted me with a hug, making me feel immediately welcome, telling me how glad she was that she finally got to meet Adam's girl. She'd wanted him to meet someone nice and he finally had.

After meeting his parents we went upstairs to the room where we would be staying. Walking down the hall I counted six doors total. The room we went into was Adam's old room. It was huge and had an in-room bath.

Like the downstairs, this room had been remodeled too and had all new furniture. I wondered if all the rooms had new furniture in them. I wondered how many bedrooms there were.

"Want to see the rest of the house?" Adam asked.

"Yes, I would." I replied turning to take the hand he was holding out for me.

Four of the other doors led to bedrooms similar to Adams in size. Each also had an in-room bath. However the furniture and theme was different in each one. One was definitely very feminine and I assumed it had been Lucy's.

The sixth door led to a ginormous game room with a pool table at one end and a dart board at the other. There was also a fully stocked bar with a drink fridge and an overstuffed sofa set and coffee tables.

Going downstairs he led me through the sitting areas and into the massive kitchen. It had everything imaginable and everything had its place. The downstairs guest bath was larger and nicer than the master bath in my apartment. Everything was dark wood and granite.

The master bedroom was downstairs, tucked away at the end of a long hall that housed a huge walk in linen closet and a huge utility room.

My favorite area was the covered stone patio in the back. It was absolutely gorgeous and large enough for an outdoor sofa set and several bistro tables that sat overlooking the in-ground pool. If I ever owned my own home I would want a porch like this. Everything was very nice, and very rich.

We went back inside and sat next to the fireplace. I noticed the logs were gas logs and the fire was turned on low. It was getting colder outside and the fire was relaxing.

"You never told me that you grew up in such a nice home." I said to Adam. I had just assumed he had come from a blue collar family like me. Now seeing the house he grew up in, it seemed unlikely. I knew that his parents were retired, but it had never occurred to me to ask what they did before retiring.

He seemed to read my expression. "Both of my parents are doctors and they made a good living when they worked and saved for a good retirement. The house had belonged to my dad's dad. When grandpa died, dad inherited the house."

"I was only five when we moved here. Over time my parents have had the entire interior remodeled. It wasn't always this nice. In fact it was pretty run down at first."

"My parents paid for my college because they believe in education, but they also believe in a good work ethic. They never just gave us money. If we needed some they would make us work for it and we never got paid before the job was done."

"It's never been about the house or the things I possess. Home had just always been where my family is. I guess that's why I never mentioned it. I didn't think it would matter to you. Does it?"

"No, of course not, I was just a little surprised and when I first came in I felt a little out of place, wondering if I was dressed okay. I worry about stuff like that. I know I shouldn't, but I do."

"You always dress beautifully, and you are never out of place as far as I'm concerned. I want you to be comfortable here." He said looking a little concerned.

I stroked the side of his face. "I am. Your mother and father are very nice and made me feel welcome right away."

"Good," he said kissing me on the forehead.

"So you didn't want to be a doctor?" I asked changing the subject.

"No, that just wasn't me. I was never into the blood and guts scene. I loved math and mom and dad didn't care what I did as long as I could support myself doing it.

I may never make the money a doctor does but I like what I do. And besides, I have a pretty hefty inheritance from my grandpa just sitting in an account, waiting for when I start my family."

I was surprised again and I'm sure my face showed it. "So you get it when you get married?"

"No, I already have it. I just don't need it now and want it to be there when it really matters. Someday I would like to build a house and get out of the apartment scene. It probably won't be as big as this, but something nice; maybe on Bainbridge if I get the position there."

There was a question in his eyes, as if he was waiting for my approval of his idea. *Why is he telling me this?* I wasn't sure what to say or how to act. For some reason I didn't feel comfortable making suggestions or decisions about money that I didn't earn; money that didn't belong to me.

"That sounds really nice. Bainbridge is beautiful," Was all I could manage.

He looked thoughtful for a moment, pushing a stray strand of hair behind my ear.

"I love you so much Drew. Tell me you know that I love you. Tell me you love me too. I suddenly feel like you're pulling away from me."

I leaned into him, kissing him tenderly. "I'm not pulling away from you. This is just a lot to take in all at once. It's a whole different side of you and I no longer know where my boundaries lie. I don't want to overstep them. But I do love you Adam, and I know that you love me." The truth was it suddenly occurred to me just how little I really knew about Adam. How could I be so in love with someone I was barely beginning to know?

Propping his feet up on an ottoman he pulled me into his lap, reclining me against his chest. "Then you should know that you are part of my life now. I want you to be involved in every aspect of it. Nothing has changed about me. I'm still the same person I was yesterday."

"Okay." I said.

He was right. Nothing about him had changed at all. Only my knowledge about him had changed. I had mixed emotions about this new knowledge too. It wasn't a bad revelation. On the contrary I should have been happy.

Adam came from a wealthy family and had some money of his own. That was good really, but part of me felt a little let down that he had not told me sooner. The rational part of me pointed out that if it were me, I'd have waited too.

Eventually the fact that I loved him and none of this even mattered won out. I loved him and he loved me. I reached up stroking his face with my hand. I couldn't see him but I felt it as he leaned his head into my touch. I couldn't ask for better than this. I'd never find a better man than Adam Knight.

His mother came into the room then and I was embarrassed to be sitting in his lap, but Adam seemed determined to keep me there. She seemed to enjoy the sight of us immensely as she stood over us smiling.

"After twenty-nine years I was afraid he was going to be a bachelor forever. I can't tell you how good it makes me feel to see him holding you in his lap. Reminds me of his father and me when we were young."

Adam squeezed me tighter against him, kissing my cheek. "Mom you know I was just waiting for the right girl to come along."

"I came to talk to you about dinner tonight. None of the other kids will be here until late tonight. Your father and I would like to take the two of you out to that seafood restaurant you like so much."

Adam looked at me. "Is seafood okay with you?"

"Sure I love seafood."

"Sounds great, what time?" Adam asked.

We left for the restaurant an hour later after a quick shower and a change of clothes. I let Adam order for me since he knew what was good on the menu and we shared off each other's plates.

I got to know his parents some and listened to stories about Adam when he was young. Apparently he was always into some kind of mischief. Being the middle child he somehow seemed to get left out of things. He was either too old or too young and it was up to him to entertain himself.

Throughout almost the entire meal Adam kept his hand on my knee, stroking across it with his thumb. By the time we got in the car to leave I was ready to explode. Adam grinned, showing off his dimple. I crossed my legs and resisted the temptation to make out like teenagers in the backseat of his parent's car.

I wasn't sure if we needed to wait up for the others that would be coming in later or not, but Rebecca assured us that they would be able to let themselves in. We were free to go to bed and we had the entire upstairs to ourselves. I was relieved. I couldn't wait to get Adam alone.

Walking into the room, Adam closed the door behind me. I heard the familiar click of the lock being turned. Then the lights went out and I was standing in total darkness. I stood waiting, listening, every sense heightened.

I heard the softest of footfalls behind me and smelled his body-wash before I felt his hands on my shoulders. His fingers traced the neckline of my dress sending shivers down my spine as they reached the zipper.

At a tormenting slow pace he unzipped the dress, following with a sensual assault of his mouth on my neck and spine. My back tingled with each slight touch sending waves of pleasure through my core. I felt him kneel as he reached the end of the zipper then felt his tongue on the small of my back.

I arched into his touch as he pulled the dress from my shoulders allowing it to pool at my feet. His hands went to my belly then slid up my body as he stood again.

With my breasts in his hands he pulled me against him; my back to his bare chest. He had already removed his shirt. Again his mouth was on my neck and I turned my head to give him better access.

His hands cupped my breast through my lacy bra, his thumbs circling my nipples, as his mouth sucked and pulled on my neck. My hands moved over his head, tangling my fingers in his hair.

"I want you." I whispered into the silence of the darkness.

He growled; his hands moving to my hips, pulling me back hard against his erection.

"Do you feel that?" He growled in my ear. "Feel how hard you make me."

One hand he splayed across my belly, the other went to my bra, pulling the band up, exposing my breasts, fingering them as he continued to grind against me.

I slipped a hand between us and firmly grasped him through his pants, feeling the hardness of his shaft. My panties were saturated from my arousal and I longed to feel him buried deep in my core.

"Do you want that?" He asked me, biting on my ear.

"Yes." I panted.

"Are you wet for me baby?"

"Yes." I said again, pushing back against him.

His hand slipped from my belly down into my panties, his fingers spreading me wide; slick from my juices.

"Oh baby." He moaned into my hair. "You are so fucking wet for me."

I ground against his fingers wanting to feel him inside me. He removed his hand and quickly unhooked my bra letting it fall to the floor.

"Come to the bed." He said leading me in the darkness across the room. "Bend over." He commanded, when I reached the edge of the bed.

I quickly complied. He knelt behind me and pulled my panties off.

"Spread your legs, I want to feel that pussy." I moved my legs apart feeling his finger slip inside me. Then I felt his hot mouth on me and almost came.

He lapped at the entrance to my core with his divine tongue while his fingers circled my swollen clit; His tongue delving deeper each time.

My body was trembling with need. I was building inside.

"Come for me baby." He said, now with two fingers inside me.

I came, biting on a pillow to keep from screaming out his name as waves of pleasure pulsated through me. He continued to pump with his fingers until the last shudder subsided then removed his hand.

I lay limp on the edge of the bed. A moment later the bedside lamp came on. I watched in eager anticipation as he unzipped his pants and removed them along with his boxers. Walking toward me, he slowly worked the length of his cock with his hand.

"Now I want you on your back."

Moisture pooled at the entrance to my body when he spoke. I couldn't get enough of him. I wanted him again - Now.

It took him two seconds to flip me over onto my back with my butt off the edge of the bed and my legs over his shoulders. Another two seconds as he slowly pushed in, filling me to capacity.

And then he started moving. I watched in the lamplight as this beautiful man made love to me. Watched as his cock moved in and out of me; watched as his abdominal muscles contracted and tightened with each thrust. I saw the rise and fall of his chest as he breathed.

He was perfect and when he was inside of me it was heaven. I had never felt so connected to someone in my life. Never had I wanted to please someone the way I wanted to please him.

I slid my hands through the sweat on his body, feeling the tension in the hard muscles of his arms. I was ready to come again already but I wanted to see his face when he came. He was building, I could tell. So I pushed him over the edge.

Tightening my pelvic muscles I squeezed down around him so tightly he could barely pull out and push back in.

"Come baby. Come now with me." I urged, squeezing around him again as he thrust.

He was unable to hold back and I watched as he fell apart between my legs even as I came with him. I saw the look of pleasure on his face, felt the tremors that moved through his body, felt the heat of his cock emptying out inside me and heard the moan that he couldn't suppress. Then I watched as he collapsed down on top of me, shattered to the core.

TWENTY

The smell of fresh bread and coffee ignited my senses, dragging me back to a state of consciousness. Adam had climbed into the bed, bringing me with him and together we fell asleep in a tangled heap of arms and legs.

Two hours later I awoke to tender kisses and the gentle nudge of his erection at my opening. I was exhausted but I wouldn't deny him. I couldn't if I'd wanted to; my body already responding to him, even from a dead sleep. I wanted him again... And again.

Now as I lie next to him every movement reminded me of where he'd been. I was sore. It had been a while since we'd gone at it all night like last night.

He snaked his arm around my waist pulling me against his chest. "Are you okay baby?"

I nodded, melting into him. I loved being so close to him. "I'm alright. A little sore and still tired but it was very worth it."

He kissed my face, brushing my hair back. "I should have given you a break. I didn't mean to abuse you. I just…I just needed you last night…I want you to know how I really feel."

I turned around in his arms. "I do know Adam, I feel the same way."

Wrapping my hair around his hand, he pulled back, holding my head in place as he ravaged my mouth. Willingly I surrendered. I felt his hunger, understood his need. His feelings were reflected in me, woven through the very fabric of my being. I had fallen into him; fallen into Adam Knight.

He stopped; panting, he rested his forehead against mine. Beneath the covers I felt his erection pulsing against my thigh. He needed me again. I didn't know if I could stand to be taken again so soon, but there was something I could do. Something I had wanted to do all night.

Pushing him onto his back I knelt beside him in the bed. He was so beautiful lying there naked. His body was pure perfection; his cock pulsing and rising off his belly; I wanted it…in my mouth.

He watched with rapt attention as I lowered my face to his belly and began to suck and lick the head of his beautiful cock. I loved the taste of his pre-cum, the musky smell of Adam and sex, and the way his cock swelled larger as I swirled my tongue around it.

Already he was on the verge of explosion. I took him deep and slid my tongue along the massive vein that fed his erection, sucking hard as I retreated down his impressive length.

Again I took him to the back of my throat, gently scraping my teeth against him as I pulled back, sucking hard again. I heard him moan as I made one last thrust into the back of my throat, then felt him explode inside my mouth. Swallowing I took it all, cleaning him with my tongue when he'd emptied completely. Spent he sank back into the softness of the mattress.

"Baby you are so fucking good to me." He gasped.

I crawled up next to him, snuggling into his side. "That's because you make it so easy." Leaning up I kissed him on the nose, "Merry Christmas baby."

The rest of the day passed in a blur. I met his other sister and both of his brothers. Jerry was married, but his wife and two youngest kids were with her mother who was ill and not expecting to make it much longer. He was going to fly out later today to be with her as well.

Anne was also married. Her husband's name was Kevin. They had a pair of six year old twins, Ashley and Elizabeth. The two were very cute with huge blue eyes. They looked a lot like their uncle Adam if you asked me.

Tom was single and very handsome, although he didn't look like anyone that I could tell. I liked him at once. Maybe because he reminded me of myself; the one dubbed the postman's child.

I thought about Lana when I met him. The two would make a cute couple I mused. But while I entertained the idea something began to niggle at the back of my mind. I just couldn't seem to place it. For the moment I didn't have time to dwell on it.

Of course Lucy and Jared were there as I'd known they would be. They had time off for the holidays and would be staying on past the New Year.

We ate dinner together then opened gifts; allowing the kids open theirs first since we were afraid they might burst from the excitement if they didn't. The adults exchanged gifts next. I don't remember too much about what anyone else received. I was so focused on Adam. I had wrapped his tickets in a small jewelry box and put some paperclips in it so it would rattle a bit. He shook it several times before finally deciding to open it.

The look on his face was priceless when he saw the pair of tickets. I'd never seen him so excited before over something. He actually let out a loud whoop as he pumped a fist in the air. Even his dad was excited about the tickets and I wondered if the other two were still available. I'd check with Davy later on.

Then Adam presented me with a gift. Nervously I opened it. I knew I would be happy with anything he gave me but I was praying it wasn't expensive. I glanced up at Adam and he looked just as nervous as I felt. As I tore away the wrapping paper a small envelope fell out. I opened it first. It was a gift card to a day spa I had seen in Seattle.

Amy and I had talked about one day going for an all-day pampering session, but that had been put on the back burner indefinitely. I didn't have that kind of money to blow. I couldn't believe it when I saw it. I loved it. I jumped up hugging him excitedly.

Adam laughed. "Open the other one too."

I'd forgotten there was still more. The card had been more than enough. Another gift was too much.

It was an iPad, another item from my list of *"wanted but not essential"* items. I was overwhelmed.

"Thank you Adam." I whispered in his ear, hugging him. "I really love them both."

"You're welcome. You should be able to do anything and everything you want to with that card."

"This is all too much you know. But thank you."

"Nothing is too much for you baby." He said kissing me softly.

TWENTY-ONE

We sat around talking for a while then I went upstairs to call home. I wanted to wish everyone a Merry Christmas.

Mom answered. "Hi honey, how are you? How is your Christmas?"

I told her all about my day with Adam and his family but she seemed a little distracted. I kept having to repeat myself. Finally I asked her if something was wrong.

"No honey, everything is fine. I'm just a little pre-occupied at the moment."

"That's okay mom, let me talk to Daniel."

"Hey squirt." He said when got on the line. "How is your Christmas? Is Adam treating you right?"

"Yes of course. I don't think you're going to have to worry about Adam. I've never been better.

Christmas is great here. Is everything okay there? Mom seemed a little off."

He was silent for a moment. When he started talking again his voice was strained. He was going for nonchalant but not doing a good job of it.

"Everything is good here Squirt. Nothing you need to worry about, just the normal craziness of our functionally dysfunctional family."

I let it drop and he seemed to relax on the other end of the line. Whatever was going on I was sure it wasn't life threatening so I resigned myself to not worry about it.

Daniel and I talked for a few more minutes before I got off the phone. "Danny, give everyone a hug for me. Tell them all I love them and Merry Christmas."

"Sure Squirt. You don't want to talk to them now?"

"No, not now, I'll talk to everyone later. I think we're about to pack up and drive home."

He was quiet again for a minute. When he started talking again the edge was back in his voice. "Drew, I just need to know. You are happy with

Adam right? No regrets with your decision to not go back to Joe? You're over him?"

I thought the questions were odd coming from Daniel but then he was pretty protective of me.

I sighed." Danny I have never been happier with a decision; have never been happier than I am right now with Adam. I'm in love with him. Honestly I am grateful that Joe left me. I would have never met Adam if he hadn't and what Adam and I have is so much more than anything I ever felt for Joe. I don't hate Joe. I hope he moves on with his life and finds someone he can be happy with. But yes, I am over him."

Daniel sighed. "Okay then, that's what I needed to hear. I love you Squirt."

"I love you too Danny."

I hung up then. Everything about that phone call was unusual. I had a bad feeling that I just couldn't shake. Something was going on at home and my family wasn't telling me about it. I finally decided if it was something important they would tell me.

In the end I shoved it to back to the recesses of my brain until I could sort it out better. For now it was Christmas. My first one with Adam and I wanted to enjoy every second of it.

Adam came up behind me. I hadn't been aware that he'd come into the room. He turned me around to face him and the look on his face; the feelings that filled the deep blue pools that were his eyes were unfathomable.

"I wasn't trying to listen in on your conversation." He said, his gaze seemingly penetrating through my exterior and into my soul. "But what you just said to your brother…I can't begin to tell you how much that means to me."

His hands were fisting in my hair, pulling my head back giving him unlimited access to my mouth and neck. He was devouring me, his tongue invading my mouth tasting and tangling with mine.

He possessed me and I loved every second of this forceful, powerful version of Adam. I soared inside feeling the strength of his arms as he lifted me, carrying me across the room, never breaking eye contact.

He carried me into the bathroom and sat me on the cool granite of the countertop. Backing up he closed and locked the door, his eyes on me the entire time. My breath hitched in my throat. I knew what was coming next and I was so ready for it.

My eyes followed his hands as they unzipped his pants and freed his massive erection. My panties were instantly soaked, my arousal at a fever pitch.

"I've got to have you again before we leave. I won't be able to make the drive home. Are you too sore?"

I shook my head. "I'll be fine...I'm not too sore."

He groaned as he moved toward me, pushing my dress up around my waist. I lifted my hips as he pulled my panties off and dropped them on the floor.

Pulling me to the edge of the cabinet, he commanded as he knelt in front of me, "Lean back baby, I want to taste you first."

He spread me wide, putting one leg over his shoulder as I leaned back, supporting my weight on my forearms. I was still tender but the warmth of his velvet tongue lapping at my entrance was soothing.

"I love how you taste. Your pussy is so fucking perfect. And it's mine." He said as he pushed a finger inside.

I moaned, feeling the invasion as he pumped it in and out a few times. "Babe you're so wet...Are you ready for this?"

I nodded, too overwhelmed with the sensation to speak.

He stood up; pushing his pants further down on his hips then pulled me against him.

"Wrap your legs around my waist." He commanded. I did as he said, holding onto his shoulders with my hands.

Placing me against the wall he used one hand to position himself at my opening, the other was under my hips. Slowly he lowered me, impaling me completely on his cock then put one hand by my head.

"Let me know if this is too much." He said as he let me adjust to the fullness.

I nodded, panting. The feeling was exquisite. Though muscles were protesting I didn't want him to stop.

"I'm ready," I said. Then he started moving.

Already muscles were tightening as my body attempted to balance itself against the wall. With each thrust I clamped down even tighter around him, feeling the friction as he moved in and out of my core.

My orgasm was already building. I wouldn't last long like this.

"Baby you're so tight right now. You're going to make me come."

At his words my head pushed back into the wall as waves of pleasure washed over me.

"Come baby." I said breathlessly.

He pumped twice more before his release tore through him, leaving him shaking. He collapsed against me, holding me pinned against the wall. I could feel his heart pounding in his chest, his breathing was ragged. With great effort he pulled out and lowered me until my feet touched the floor, and then sank to the ground bringing me with him.

We sat there for a few minutes, neither of us speaking. We were physically and mentally drained from all the sex we'd had in the last twenty-four hours. I was glad we had a few days to recuperate before going back to work. The way I felt right now I could sleep right through to the New Year.

With our bags packed and ready, we said our goodbyes to his family, promising to come back and visit soon. It had been a good trip. Adam was fortunate to have family so close. Exhausted, we climbed into the car for the drive home.

As much as I enjoyed meeting his family I was still glad to be home. I ran us a tub of hot foamy water and we both melted into the liquid heat, allowing it to soothe the soreness from our muscles.

When the water started getting cold we got out, dried off, and fell into bed. I was asleep instantly, dragged from my body into a realm where sounds couldn't reach my ears and light couldn't reach my eyes. I was dead to the world.

Adam lie awake for a few minutes watching the gentle rise and fall of Drew's breathing. As soon as her head had hit the pillow she had been sound asleep. He was exhausted too from the weekend events but had a lot on his mind at the moment.

He laughed at himself as he thought about it. The weekend events were specifically sex, sex, and more awesome sex. He couldn't help himself it seemed. He had needed her more than anything and she had not denied him.

It wasn't the first time they'd made love all night, but it was the first time they'd carried it over all day the next day too. He knew it had to do with the overwhelming feelings he'd had when talking to her about being in his life. And then again, hearing her talking to Daniel about him and how much she loved him.

He'd felt like the Grinch when he walked into the room. His heart must have grown three times as big because it had suddenly lodged in his throat. That wasn't the only thing that had grown either.

Just thinking about it made him get hard again. He'd never been with anyone that affected him like this and he wasn't about to let her go. He wanted to make this permanent, as soon as possible.

In just a couple of weeks he'd be moved in with her, but he wanted more. He wanted to get married and find a house together and someday have babies with her. She would be such a beautiful mother.

Watching her just a few moments more he couldn't stand not touching her any longer. Moving closer to her he gently pulled her against him, cradling her in his arms. Now he could go to sleep breathing in her shampoo and the smell of everything Drew.

He closed his eyes and drifted off immediately, dreaming of him and Drew, a little boy with curly, brown hair and big green eyes and a house on the Sound.

I woke sometime in the night with Adam draped over me like ivy, softly snoring. I was still tired and would have gladly gone back to sleep but my increasingly full bladder was driving me from the bed. Careful not to wake him, I eased out from his arms and legs and hurried off to the bathroom.

I was washing my hands when I heard him talking. Going back into the bedroom I realized he was talking in his sleep. His hands were groping the covers and he was calling my name. His eyes were open but looked glassy and confused.

Quickly I climbed back into bed. "I'm here Adam." I said taking his hand. He grabbed it, pulling me against him and once more wrapped himself around me.

"Don't leave me baby." He mumbled, nuzzling his nose in my hair.

"I won't leave you Adam." I whispered, as I drifted back to sleep.

It was ten o'clock before I finally woke up again. I could hear Adam in the kitchen making a pot of coffee. A few minutes later he came into the bedroom with two mugs of the hot liquid. He was so cute with his tousled curls and pajama pants I couldn't help but smile and stare.

He sat down on the bed next to me. "Enjoying the view?"

"Uh huh," I nodded.

He smiled revealing that gorgeous dimple and even white teeth. "I could strip for you." He said, untying the drawstrings on his pants in a dramatic movement. "But then I'd expect a pole dance from you."

"Oh, I forgot." I said reaching into the drawer of my nightstand, retrieving his other gift. "This was for you for Christmas but I forgot to give it to you last night."

He raised an eyebrow. "You already gave me a gift."

"I know." I smiled. "This is just…well open it."

He untied the ribbon and opened the small album. I heard him suck in air as his eyes fell on the first picture. Slowly he flipped the pages, his fingers gently touching each one as he studied them.

"Come here." He said pulling me into his lap, kissing me tenderly. "I'm glad you didn't give this to me last night or you wouldn't have gotten any sleep."

I laughed. "I'm afraid you'd of had to have been into necrophilia to do anything last night."

Reaching over I picked up the cup of coffee he'd brought me. "So what are your plans for today?"

The office was closed through the New Year so we were both off work. We would be gearing up for tax season soon enough and everyone would be getting tons of overtime.

"Spending time with you, what do you want to do?"

"I was actually thinking of getting all my stuff moved to one side of the closet. I thought maybe we could start moving some of your stuff now if you wanted to.

"Okay, maybe we can get some boxes for the stuff I won't need. Mom and dad have that big storage room. They said I could put whatever I needed to in it."

We worked a few hours every day for the next three days getting his clothing and personal effects moved downstairs. Other things we boxed up to store at his parents. The furniture and bigger items we'd worry about later.

Friday at noon we took a break, stopping for lunch. Adam had gone down the street to pick up some soup and sandwiches for us when my phone rang. It was Lana.

"Hey what's up?" I said answering the phone. Lana hardly ever called.

"Are you busy?" She asked. She sounded a little nervous on the other end.

"No, just going to eat some lunch. Why is something wrong?"

"I need to talk to you about something if you have a minute to talk. If not I can call back later." I could tell by her voice that it wasn't something she really wanted to talk about; which probably meant it couldn't wait.

"I can talk now." I said.

"I'd rather be talking to you in person than over the phone, but I don't want mom to tell you first so I don't have a choice." She paused for a minute. "I've been seeing Joe. We've been dating for a few weeks now and I want to keep seeing him, but I don't want you and me to have a problem because of it."

I went to sit down and nearly missed the stool, catching myself before I hit the floor. Her news knocked the wind out of me. I was prepared for just about anything, but this. My mind was reeling. I had questions but I also wanted to warn her away from him. A thousand thoughts tumbled through my brain leaving me in a tailspin.

She continued. "He had come into the shop a couple of times. I think the first few times were to find out about you, but after you told him you were with someone else it was more just to talk."

"We started meeting for lunches and then some dinners…and I know that you probably hate him and that you're going to tell me not to see him…but I really think…I think I'm in love with him."

Her last words finally brought me out of my stupor and I found my voice again. I suddenly realized what must have been happening back home on Christmas Day, and the reason for Daniel's strange questions. He had known what was about to happen and wanted to know how I would feel about it.

How did I feel about it? Joe had hurt me deeply, but I didn't hate him. The truth was he wasn't a bad person. It was just the way he left me that I felt so wronged. He could have done things differently but that wouldn't have kept me from being hurt. In the end it really didn't matter.

I kept saying I hoped he'd find someone he could be happy with…But my sister?

"I don't hate him Lana. I think maybe I did at first for leaving me, but I got over it."

"You…you don't still have feelings for him do you? If you see him around will you be okay?"

"I will be fine." I managed to say, "It might be a little weird, we did live together for four years, but no, I don't have any feelings for him." She was quiet on the other end.

"Lana, I just want you to be careful. I'm going to try not to judge him because people change and just because it wasn't meant to be for us, doesn't mean it's not for you."

"I won't have a problem with him unless he hurts you. I do wish you had talked to me without being forced by mom and Daniel though."

"It wasn't mom and Danny, it was Joe. He said he didn't want to hurt you again…didn't want you to think he was trying to get at you. He's been asking for weeks, trying to make sure you're really happy with Adam before we said anything. That's why he wouldn't come home with me for Thanksgiving; that and the fact that I hadn't even told mom yet." She sounded like she was about to cry.

I honestly didn't know what to say to that. Maybe Joe really did care for her. Regardless, Lana apparently cared for him and she was on the phone asking for permission to be with the person she cared about. Somehow I had to get past who that person was.

I wanted to tell her no. Not because I still had feelings for Joe or because I hated him, but because I didn't want her to get hurt like I did. But deep inside I knew that was something she would have to take a chance on if she really cared for him, which she apparently did.

Inside I was at war with myself. How could I know Joe and my sister wouldn't have the same kind of love Adam and I had? I couldn't, and despite what I felt like saying I knew I didn't have that right. I took a deep breath. This was probably the hardest thing I'd ever had to say to someone. I sighed.

"Lana you are my sister and I love you. I don't want anything, or anyone to come between us. If you care for Joe and want to be with him then that has to be your decision. I won't try to make it for you either way. My life now is with Adam and I will do my best to get along with Joe if the two of you are together. It sounds like he is trying on his end and I will do the same – for you."

Lana was silent for a long moment before I realized she was sobbing on the other end of the line. When she finally started talking again it was with broken breaths.

"I love you too sis. Thank you for this."

I was distracted momentarily as Adam came in carrying our lunch. He saw the look on my face and stopped in front of me.

"I love you too Lana. I need to get off the phone now. I'll talk to you later."

"Okay, bye."

As I hung up the phone, Adam pulled me into his arms. "Anything you want to talk about?"

I pressed my face in to his chest, willing myself not to cry. "I just found out why Danny was asking me all those questions at Christmas." I paused for a moment taking a deep breath. "It seems that Lana has been seeing Joe…they're seeing each other. She was calling to ask me if it was okay."

"What did you tell her?"

"That it was not my decision to make…that I wouldn't stand in her way if that was what she wanted."

"Are you alright with your decision?"

The question surprised me and I suddenly realized that I was. I was okay. The sky wasn't falling and the person I cared for the most stood holding me in his arms. Life for me was good.

I smiled up at him. "Yes…yes I am. Let's eat, I'm starving."

TWENTY-TWO

New Year's Eve Adam and I sat up together watching the party in Madison Square Gardens on TV. We celebrated with a kiss and a glass of champagne before going to bed.

It had been a busy week for us moving the last of Adam's stuff from his apartment to his parent's storage building. We kept his couch, putting in the study since it would make out into a bed. Thankfully Davy had been there to help with the heavy stuff.

He was officially moved in with me. Although he'd not stayed at his place in weeks, having his stuff here gave me a sense of permanence. I loved it.

The rest of the month at work, was spent closing books for our clients whose year ended in December, and printing out W-2s and W-3s for everyone that had employees. From now until April fifteenth we would be buried in bookwork and tax preparation.

I was glad that Adam had scheduled off some time in February. After Christmas I had managed to pick up the other two tickets for the super bowl. I had talked to Adam and decided he should do a guy's trip and take his dad along. Davy was going along and I'd given the last ticket to Danny.

I was going to be too busy at work anyway to take time off. Davy had agreed to go since I would be able to go with Gloria to her Ob appointment that week.

As it got closer to the time he would be flying out, Adam got noticeably more and more excited, but he was also apprehensive.

"Are you sure you're okay with me going off with the guys?" He asked me for the hundredth time.

I smiled and kissed him." Yes, it was my idea, remember?" Then I added. "But I'll miss you like hell when you're gone and I'll expect a call every night." They would only be gone two days and two nights but I was already feeling it and he wasn't even gone yet.

"I'll miss you too babe." He said squeezing my bum.

The sound of a horn blasting announced the arrival of Davy, who was driving them to the airport.

"Have fun and be careful. Tell your dad and Danny hello for me." I said as he climbed into Davy's truck. They would meet his dad at the airport and meet Daniel at the hotel in New Orleans.

As soon as he left I changed and went to the gym then spent the rest of the afternoon at the spa getting my nails and waxing done. Amy and Gloria met me at the spa and we all went out to dinner afterward.

Gloria was steadily getting bigger and more uncomfortable. She still had six weeks to go but she looked like she might pop at any moment. Her feet had started swelling and she complained that an octopus had taken up residence in her belly.

For the first time since I'd met her she wasn't wearing anything but eyeliner and her hair was pulled back in a ponytail. Not that she looked bad, she just seemed tired.

"I hope I don't embarrass you as much as I eat these days. I just can't seem to get enough food evah." She said walking into the restaurant.

I waved a hand dismissively. "It takes a lot more than that to embarrass me. Eat what you want."

We were seated at a booth next to a window and I let Gloria sit on the end since she barely fit behind the table. The entire time she had to assume a reclined position or the baby kicked so bad she was miserable.

"What time is your appointment Monday?" I asked knowing I would need to leave work thirty minutes before to pick her up.

"Two o'clock." She said. "It's the first one after their lunch so we should get in pretty fast."

I nodded. "I'll pick you up around one forty."

After dinner I went home to soak in the tub and wait for Adam to call me. Amy and Gloria would come over tomorrow to watch the game at my place.

After seeing Gloria tonight I wondered if she should be driving at all. There wasn't much room between her belly and the steering wheel. Maybe I should pick her up tomorrow.

Adam called to let me know they'd all made it in. They were going to get something to eat. I felt better knowing they'd arrived safely. I hung up the phone and slid into the hot water that was waiting for me.

The next day I busied myself with laundry and housework until it was almost time for the game.

Amy showed up around four and Gloria came a few minutes later.

I had offered to pick her up but she had declined saying "I can't tie my own shoes, shave my own legs, and sometimes I can't even step into my own panties. I can still drive though so I'm gonna keep doin' it till I can't."

I was glad that she didn't have to climb stairs to get to my apartment. She was waddling so badly she looked a bit unsteady and I just knew if she fell she'd bust open like a ripe watermelon.

We sat and talked more than we watched the game but it did draw our attention when the lights went out at the stadium. Adam started texting me when that happened. Fortunately they were sitting on the side that still had power.

We didn't watch the whole game. Gloria was exhausted and Amy and I had to get up early for work the next day. I knew Adam would give me a play by play re-cap anyway. He would be home tomorrow evening.

The next day I worked until noon then left to get Gloria. We had decided to eat lunch before her appointment. After that I drove to her doctor's office. We didn't have to wait long before they called her.

"Come on back with me." She said heaving herself up from the chair. "They're just gonna weigh and measure me again today. Then she'll tell me I'm now the size of a small cow but my udder is on the wrong end."

I laughed and so did the nurse we were following. The nurse had her step onto the scale then measured her girth and took her vital signs. After that we waited for the doctor in the exam room.

Gloria's doctor was a young woman who appeared to be in her early thirties. She smiled as she entered the room.

"How are you and the baby doing today?"

Gloria groaned. "The baby's fine but I'm ready for her to be on the outside now."

"So you feel like you're going to have a girl then?"

"I feel like I'm having an octopus," Gloria corrected. "I swear this baby has eight arms and legs and they all kick and punch around like Jackie Chan. I'm just miserable."

The doctor smiled. "Well, you don't have too much longer to go. Let's listen to the heartbeat."

Gloria leaned back on the exam table as the doctor spread some goop on the Doppler. She felt around on Gloria's belly for a minute, a puzzled look on her face.

Grabbing her stethoscope she listened to one area then another. "Oh my," She said suddenly.

Gloria tensed. "What is it? Is something wrong?"

The doctor smiled, taking out the Doppler again. "It seems that someone was hiding something, and that something is actually someone." She placed the Doppler against Gloria's belly. "Listen." She said. A distinct rapid heartbeat was amplified on the Doppler.

Gloria breathed a sigh of relief. Then the doctor moved the Doppler over to the other side. Another distinct, rapid heartbeat, but this one was somewhat slower that the first.

Gloria looked confused. "Is that my heartbeat down there?"

"No, that would be our hide and seek player. Baby number two. From the heart beat I'd guess a boy, but we won't know for sure until they get here."

"They," Gloria repeated numbly.

337

"Yes, there are definitely two babies in there. No wonder you feel like there are eight arms and legs, there are. This changes things though. We need to watch you a little closer. Sometimes these twins want to come a little early. You're doing great though. If they decided to come today it would be alright."

Gloria had suddenly turned white and I thought she might pass out. Not knowing what to do I squeezed her hand.

"Are you alright?" I asked.

She took a deep breath. "I wasn't expecting this but yeah I'll be fine. Twins huh…Davy is gonna freak!"

I drove her home and walked her to the front door.

"Is there anything I need to do before I go?"

"No, I'm good. I'm going to take a nap now." She paused for a minute before going inside. "I don't want to tell Davy until he gets back home, but if you talk to Adam, tell him not to let Davy do anything stupid between here and there. I need him back in one piece."

I went back to work after that. I had left a ton of paperwork on my desk and wanted to at least get it put away so I could start fresh tomorrow.

Riding up in the elevator I thought about Adam and sent a quick text.

Whatever you do, make sure Davy gets home alive and well. See you tonight. Love you.

I didn't wait for an answer but hurried back to my desk. I had two hours left to work so I did as much as I could. By the time four-thirty rolled around I had finished the stack. Neatening my desk I got up and headed for the time clock.

I was startled when I turned around to find Ned standing behind me. He rarely said two words to me anymore since the incident at the Halloween party. I think Adam had scared him to death, but he had been in a better mood lately.

Now he stood with his arms folded and a smug look on his face.

"I think you should know that your boyfriend is finally getting just what he deserves."

I should have let it drop and walked away but curiosity got the better of me. "And what would that be?" I asked.

"I happen to know from a very reliable source, my girlfriend Tabitha, that Adam will not be getting the promotion he thinks he's entitled to. And just so you know. It's because he just can't keep his hands or lips off of you at work like professional people do." He said exaggerating the word professional."

Ned continued talking, his voice getting louder and higher as he continued, his anger toward Adam spilling out of his mouth. A small crowd had gathered around the time clock listening and others were craning their necks from their cubicles to see what the commotion was about.

"I'm just so glad that he is finally getting put in his place. I'll bet your little romance won't last too much longer once he figures out that you kept him from an awesome promotion. After all it was you that told the old man himself that the two of you were together. Ironic don't you think?"

I was suddenly ill. I couldn't believe what I was hearing. Ned couldn't have hurt me worse if he'd kicked me in the gut. The fact that he stood there smirking at me made it even worse.

I wanted to run out of the building and throw up. What he said had thrown me for a loop, but I wasn't about to give the asshole the satisfaction of knowing just how badly I was affected. Instead I just looked at him with a cool glare and pretended not to know what he was talking about.

"I'm not sure exactly what it is you think you know about Adam's business, but I'm sure it's far less than you're making it out to be. I'm also sure that the only reason you are saying this is because Adam isn't here. You wouldn't have the balls to say that to a man so you waited until he was out of town to harass his girlfriend. I hope Tabitha finds out what a pathetic prick you are before she makes the mistake of falling for you."

With that I turned on my heels and left. I was so upset that I barely heard Amy call my name. She caught up to me by the elevators and pulled me aside.

"Are you okay hon?" She asked, anger firing from her eyes. "I had just walked up when he started that back there."

I shook my head looking around to make sure no one was near. "I think I'm going to be sick. I need to get out of here."

She pressed the button to call the car then turned to me. I'll go down with you and make sure he doesn't bother you anymore. I've got something I have to do but I can stop by if you want me to."

The door opened and we got in. Amy quickly pushed the button to shut the door, not wanting anyone to join us.

I shook my head. "Adam will be home soon. I guess I should to talk to him. I may as well face the music now."

"Just what do you mean by that?" Amy asked in disbelief. "You can't possibly be listening that asshole. There is no way Adam would break up with you for something like this."

I shrugged my shoulders. "If the rest of what he says is true, then it is my fault. I did talk to Larry at the Christmas party." The elevator door opened into the lobby and we stepped out.

Amy shook her head. "Go home and talk to Adam. You'll see I'm right. Call me if you need me. I'll be leaving here shortly." Then she turned and got back on the elevator.

Fear and nausea washed over me in waves. I was on the verge of tears all the way home. I was angry at myself for talking to Larry. How could I have been so stupid? I just never thought he would use the information against Adam.

How could I have messed up such an awesome opportunity for him? If it wasn't for me and my mouth, Adam would still have a chance at the promotion.

By the time I got home I really had to throw up. Bursting through the door I ran to the toilet and heaved my guts up. I didn't even realize that Adam was home.

I stood over the toilet shaking and crying.

"Baby are you okay? Why are you crying?"

I whirled around at his voice, startled that he was there. One look at my face and he grabbed my arms, panic in his eyes.

"What happened Drew? Did someone do something to you?"

Another wave of nausea washed over me and I pulled away, running back to the toilet, heaving up what was left of my lunch.

After a minute I went to the sink and shakily washed my face, rinsing my mouth out.

Adam handed me a towel then picked me up and carried me into the living room.

"I want to know what is going on now. Please tell me."

I almost choked on the lump that came up in my throat but I managed to tell him everything. I watched as the expression on his face grew angrier and angrier by the minute. I couldn't take it any longer. I knew he must hate me now. Ned had been right. I'd screwed this up for him.

"I'm so sorry." I sobbed. "I'll understand if you want to break up with me. I know I messed this up for you."

"What?" He asked, incredulously. "How could you think that? I'm not angry at you at all. What I want is to go to Ned's house and pound his head into the concrete for harassing you the minute I left town. That sorry mother-fucker! I'm fucking tired of his bullshit."

Adam rarely cursed, but when he did it was because he'd been pushed past his limit.

"But it is my fault. I shouldn't have talked to Larry." I said feebly.

Adam shook his head and pulled me close. "Don't ever talk or think about us breaking up again. I wasn't looking for that job when it was offered to me and if I don't get it…well, there will be other opportunities."

"But I was looking for you…I've been looking for you all my life and there's no way in hell I'm going to let you get away from me. I'm just sorry I wasn't there to protect you today."

"I don't want you to feel bad about this. You didn't do anything I wouldn't have done. I'm not trying to hide our relationship, never have and never will. I don't regret one kiss that I've given you, in the elevator at work or anywhere and I'll do it again tomorrow in front of the whole damn company."

"Ned can kiss my ass if he thinks he's going to ruin anything for us. I won't allow that to happen. But baby, you've got to stop listening to that prick. You should know me better than that. It hurts that you would think so low of me, that you'd think I would leave you over something like this."

I started crying again. He was right. Amy had tried to reason with me. Why did I keep listening to Ned?

"Shhhh, stop crying now, it's okay," He said smoothing my hair from my face. "Tonight is going to be a good night. I'm going to feed you, and then I'm going to take you to bed and make love to you all night. I've spent two very long, lonely nights away and I need you."

"I want you too." I said as he lifted my chin, kissing me softly on the lips.

What was it going to take to make me completely trust him the way he deserved? He had done nothing wrong, but twice now I had immediately expected him to bail on me. Was it because of what Joe had done?

I decided to do better from now on. Adam wasn't Joe. He wasn't going to just up and walk out someday. I could trust him. I nuzzled my face into his chest, letting his powerful arms comfort me.

"Now," he said, "I got Davy home safely and in one piece. What happened with Gloria?"

His question reminded me that the entire day wasn't bad, forcing a smile to my lips. "The doctor found another baby today. Gloria's pregnant with twins!" I said.

TWENTY-THREE

The next day the office was buzzing about what had happened the afternoon before. Everywhere I went people were talking in hushed tones. Twice people came to me to ask how I was doing.

It became apparent that several people had witnessed the whole conversation and had gone directly to Randy about it, and then to everyone else in the office.

Ned spent the entire morning being counseled for his inappropriate behavior toward another coworker, and speaking to them in a degrading manner in front of their peers.

He was also reprimanded for 'leaking' alleged sensitive information about another person's employment status that he was neither privy to nor authorized to deliver such information.

In the end he was placed on six months' probation for his actions. If he had another offense within that six month period he could be subject to termination.

At noon I was summonsed to Larry's office. I was afraid, not knowing why I was being called, but became even more nervous when I saw Adam already seated in front of his desk.

Larry offered me a broad smile. "Come in please, have a seat." He said pointing toward the chairs. His smile eased my nerves some but not completely. I still found myself holding my breath.

I moved closer and sat next to Adam who also looked a bit nervous.

"I'm not going to beat around the bush." Larry started immediately. "I'm sure you are both wondering why I've asked you to come to my office."

I nodded, unable to find my voice.

Larry continued. "As you both are aware, there was an unfortunate incident yesterday afternoon that has the whole building buzzing. I've called you both in to do damage control. I want to apologize for what happened and fill you in on the facts."

"It seems that a small amount of information was inadvertently passed to Ned and he took it grossly out of context then used it for his own personal reasons. For that he has had disciplinary action brought against him."

"I also want you to know, Drew, that nothing you were told yesterday was correct. I felt I should explain the situation and I wanted you here when I spoke to Adam. I've already asked Adam and he has assured me it is alright to discuss this information in front of you."

"I don't want you to feel that what you told me had a negative impact towards Adam. That is not the case at all."

He then turned his attention to Adam. "Adam, when I spoke with you last year I mentioned that I had a couple of projects I was looking forward to getting started on."

"One of the projects was the Bainbridge office. I had come to you because I knew that you could do the job and I felt that you would be the best man for the position."

"The job would be starting from scratch with a completely new crew and building from the ground up. It would mean hours and hours of overtime and pouring your life into it; something that would not be difficult for a single young man."

"The other office would be positioned further south. At the time I had planned to relocate staff from this office. It would operate as a satellite, reaching clients whose businesses are in that area. However the startup would be easy. Everyone would already know their jobs. It would simply be a new location made up of existing employees."

"I had wanted you to take the office that would be the most work. I know you and have a lot of respect for your abilities. I knew that you could build that business, probably better than anyone else I might put there. But that was before I found out how serious your relationship had become."

Adam started to speak, but Larry held up his hand. "Please, just let me finish before you say anything."

Adam conceded and Larry continued.

"Adam you know how I feel about family. There is nothing more important, in my way of thinking, and I want to make it quite clear that I am not opposed to the two of you being in a relationship."

"I am opposed to putting a new relationship in a position that would almost certainly result in failure. It's one thing for a single man to take on a new start-up. It's a totally different task when you're trying to balance home life with work."

"Adam I've watched you now for eight years and this is the first time I've ever seen you in a serious relationship. Watching the two of you at the party in December reminded me of my wife and me forty years ago. I want the two of you to succeed."

"That is why when I realized how serious things had gotten for you that I started making changes. I still want you to take the Bainbridge office, but not for new start up."

"It will make better sense to open the satellite branch on Bainbridge. We already have a customer base on the island. Their service will go un-interrupted. If I decide to move forward with the south office I will give it to Thomas. Though he wasn't my first choice for a ground-up build, he is capable."

Larry leaned back in his chair. His elbows rested on the desk in front of him as he tented his fingers. He looked thoughtfully at me then at Adam.

"Well, what do you think?" He asked. "I know it won't be as challenging but it is still a great opportunity. Are you still interested?"

I looked at Adam expectantly. I was ecstatic that he hadn't been passed over for the promotion like I'd thought. He also looked relieved.

"What is the ETA for the opening?" He asked.

Larry smiled. "We've had to push it back a bit. Mid-July is when I anticipate. Of course I'm sure you have other questions such as pay etc., but I assure you it will be well worth your consideration."

Adam nodded. "I am interested and I would like to discuss the particulars of the position."

"Great!" Larry said standing up behind his desk. Adam and I also stood. Larry came around the desk to shake Adam's hand.

"I will set up a meeting with the board so that we can go over details with you. I'll call and let you know the date and time of the meeting."

Larry turned to me, taking my hand between his two. "Once again Drew, I apologize for the scene yesterday afternoon. That is not how I like to run my business but occasionally situations arise. I'll do my best to make sure it doesn't happen again."

I nodded. "Thank you. Although I don't put you at blame for the incident I appreciate your concern."

We left Larry's office together. Adam seemed calm and collected but the excitement shined in his eyes. He pulled my hand to his mouth, kissing my knuckles.

"Let's go grab some lunch." He said, "We can talk about this while we eat."

"Alright, but I need to run down and get my purse from my desk."

Adam went with me to get my purse, making his presence known on the floor. He didn't say anything but I know he wanted Ned to see that we were still together, and still happy despite the things he'd said.

I was cooking dinner that evening when I got a call from Gloria. She started to say something then stopped mid-sentence. There was a long pause where all I could hear was her breathing.

"Are you okay," I asked concerned, "Do you need me to come over?"

Finally she began speaking again. "I think it's time. I don't know where the hell Davy went but I need to get to the hospital?"

"I'm on my way," I said.

I didn't waste a second, pulling dinner off the stove and grabbing my purse. "Gloria's in labor," I told Adam, "and she needs a ride."

Adam grabbed his phone and keys. "I'll come with you. Where is Davy?"

"She didn't know where he is, that's why she called me."

We climbed into Adam's car and drove to get Gloria. She looked exhausted and her face and lips were swollen. She said her contractions were coming every eight minutes. Just as she finished her sentence, she was driven almost to her knees as another one hit her. I went to her bathroom and grabbed a stack of towels in case we didn't make it to the hospital.

We let the pain pass then helped her to the car. I got in the back seat with her and tried to call Davy. Each time my call just went to voicemail. I sent multiple texts to him, hoping he'd look at his phone. I was starting to be concerned that something had happened to him.

Her contractions were now only five minutes apart and each time her body was racked with pain. I had to remind her to breath. We were almost to the hospital. Adam was flying low with the pedal to the floor.

"I think I'm gonna be sick." She said, as her uterine muscles started to relax again. I spied an empty fountain drink cup and held it for her. Instantly her stomach began to revolt from the pain, heaving up the yellow-green bile that filled it.

Adam did his best to focus on the road, but he looked like he was turning green in the rearview mirror. I had grown up with this kind of stuff. It wasn't my favorite thing to do, but I had a stomach of steel.

When she was done I found the plastic lid and put it on, securing the cup in the drink holder. With any luck it wouldn't get knocked over.

Finally, after what seemed an eternity, we pulled up to the hospital.

"My doctor said just come up to the fourth floor and check in there. She'll be waiting on me."

Going in first, I spotted a wheelchair near the reception desk and wheeled it out for Gloria. Together Adam and I helped her out of the car. She was racked with a wave of pain as she stood, and her water broke, sending a deluge into her shoes.

I grabbed a couple of the towels for her to sit on, not waiting for this one to pass. Wrapping her with towels, we managed to get her to the fourth floor, labor and delivery ward.

Her doctor met us at the front desk and Gloria was whisked away to a room at the end of the hall. We were told that once she was changed and placed on monitors we would be able to go in. Twenty minutes later a nurse came to tell us we could see her now.

I was surprised when I entered the room. It looked like a hotel suite and it was huge for a hospital room. The babies would be delivered right here. Gloria was hooked up to an IV and had a funny looking belt around her belly. She told me it was tracking the babies' heart beats and her contractions.

The doctor had performed a pelvic exam and said she still had a way to go. She wasn't dilated far enough yet. I had expected the babies to pop out on the ride over, but I was glad they didn't. Gloria looked worried about Davy but she was in too much pain to say much about it.

Adam decided to go to the waiting room to try to reach him again. He wasn't gone but twenty minutes when he reappeared.

"Davy is on his way now. He said he was out trying to find you some chicken and dumplings that you asked for and his phone was set to vibrate."

Gloria looked relieved. "I forgot about telling him that."

"He's got your little suitcase you packed. He should be here in just a few minutes."

"Oh, I forgot about that too. I hope he hurries. I want him to be here when the babies come."

"The doctor tells me you should have plenty of time." Adam said.

The words were no sooner out of his mouth than Gloria was bowled over in another contraction. My heart broke for her as she let out a desperate cry. Her face was contorted in pain and sweat was beading on her forehead. I gave her my hand to squeeze and she nearly broke my fingers.

I was watching her monitor and this contraction was much stronger than the ones she'd had before. It was like having my own little Richter scale here in the room. I hoped she didn't have too many more bad ones like this.

"Something's wrong," she cried as the contraction finally passed. "I feel something." She moved her leg and pulled her gown back. The baby's head was more than crowning.

"Shit - Adam get the doctor now." I ordered. "She's having this baby."

Adam was out the door and two seconds later the doctor and nurse came in. Gloria would not let me leave so I put on one of the hats and masks I was given. Her doctor was just as calm and relaxed as she could be as she had Gloria roll onto her back.

"Oh my," she said as she pulled back the gown. "You didn't want to wait did you," she said gently to the baby. "Well, let's get you the rest of the way out."

Gloria started crying. "Where's Davy, he's supposed to be here."

There was a suddenly commotion at the door as Davy busted through. "Baby, I'm here Gloria." He said panting.

The doctor looked up. "Alright, now we can rock and roll. Let's get daddy a mask and gown."

I gave up my spot next to Gloria and stood across the room where I could still see. One good push and baby number one joined us in the room. It was a girl and the doctor wrapped her in a pink blanket handing her off to a waiting nurse.

"Ok Gloria," the doctor said. With your next contraction give me another good push. Not too hard. We'll get baby number two."

I glanced up at Davy. He was looking pretty pale. I hoped he didn't faint. Gloria seemed to have gotten her second wind.

As the next contraction started, Gloria began pushing. It didn't take long for baby number two to poke its head out. Another good push and baby was delivered right into the doctor's hands.

"Well would you look at that," she said smiling, "another girl."

"You hear that Davy?" Gloria was saying. "I told you it was girls." But Davy couldn't answer. He was passed out on the floor…

TWENTY-FOUR

The next two weeks were crazy for Adam. He was called into one meeting after another discussing the start-up of the Bainbridge office. Larry brought in some consultants one morning and they spent the entire day in the conference room. At the end of the first week Adam had accepted the offer for the new position.

Adam apologized to me each night when he came in dead tired. We had started taking separate vehicles due to meetings he was expected to attend. This was only supposed to go on for a week or two at the most. Already I was weary of them.

Suddenly it seemed I never saw Adam and when I did he was preoccupied and distracted. I tried to be patient knowing it would get back to normal soon, but after a while I seriously began to wonder if it would.

I found myself looking forward to talking to Otis. He had been around for two days because one of the elevators was acting up again. Twice now I had gotten tired of waiting for the one working car and taken the stairs down after work.

Both times, just when the office was closing, I passed an attractive young woman making her way up as I was going down. I had no idea who she was, where she was going or why she was entering the building after hours, but I really didn't give it much thought.

That second day of only one elevator Adam came home even later than normal. I waited dinner for him, cooking it only after he'd called to say he'd only be twenty minutes. An hour and a half later his dinner was cold and I was pissed.

I was truly glad that Larry had chosen not to put Adam over the other project but even with the '*less demanding*' position I was feeling downright neglected. Adam was at work all day and all night it seemed.

When he finally made it home he was in a great mood, which made me even more upset. And to make matters worse he smelled like a woman's cologne.

It was all over his hands and when I mentioned it he just waved it off. He said he'd had to handle some portfolios that supposedly had scented hand lotion on them from one of the women. I didn't know there was a woman board member.

He made it up to me that night. We made love then spent an hour or more just talking and making plans to have lunch together the next day. I really needed the time with him. I was starting to get paranoid. All of my insecurities were resurfacing as he spent less and less time with me.

The next day I was in a better mood than I had been all week, until Adam called to cancel our lunch date. Some meeting had come up. He promised he'd make it up to me with dinner tonight, but still I was hurt. It was my birthday and he didn't even remember. Not that I had ever really celebrated. With my family it was just a cake and a meal and maybe some friends to eat cake with. Still I had hoped that he would at least remember.

I sulked through a lunch with Amy then decided to drop by his office on the way back.

As I exited the one working elevator heading to his office I saw the woman I'd passed in the stairwell leaving Adam's office. Sirens were blaring in my head as I looked at her, trying to figure out who she was.

I didn't miss the sly smile that spread across her mouth when she saw me. The kind of smile that says *I've got a secret that you don't know.* I didn't miss the scent of her perfume either; the same one that Adam had all over his hands last night. My stomach tied into a thousand knots. My worst fears were coming true all over again.

I saw the woman duck into Connie's office as I turned into Adam's. He looked a little alarmed to see me and he quickly slid some stuff off his desk and into a drawer.

"Who was that?" I asked in a very accusing tone.

"What do you mean?" He asked, going for innocent and failing miserably.

"The woman who just left your office," I stated angrily. "Is she the reason you couldn't have lunch with me?"

Adam looked at me coolly. "She just brought some more portfolios over for me to look over. That's all. You're not getting *catty* on me are you?" He asked attempting a smile.

"Catty is what I get when another woman messes with my man. It's something entirely different when my man is messing with another woman." I said bluntly.

Adam looked shocked. "Baby you know me better than that. What's gotten into you?"

I stepped closer to him and took his hand bringing it to my face. "What's gotten into me?" I asked raising my eyebrows, "Maybe the fact that I never see you anymore. You work late every night and now when you come home you smell like another woman. And then I see her coming from your office after you cancel lunch with me and you smell like her again."

I turned to leave but Adam was around his desk instantly, shutting his office door.

"Drew, don't walk out like this." He said pinning me between him and the door. "You know I love you. I would never do anything that would hurt you. You're jumping to conclusions again and blowing things out of proportion."

I wanted to believe him so badly and feeling his body pressed against mine was what I had craved for the past two weeks. My body melted into his as his mouth claimed mine. A moan escaped my lips as he pressed his hips against me, my body betraying me. I wanted him.

"Baby you've got to trust me. I'm not Joe. Please stop comparing me to him."

"Then tell me who she is." I said

"She's just a girl that has been called in to help around here. She is nothing to me. You are the only woman I am interested in. She wears a lot of perfume and it gets all over the portfolios."

"Did you have lunch with her?"

"No. I told you I had an important meeting. And I promise we'll get out for dinner tonight, just you and me. Please don't be angry with me. I know these last few weeks have been hard on you. They've been hard on me too, but I promise I will make it up to you."

I sighed leaning against his solid chest. He relaxed and wrapped his arms around me, stroking up and down my spine.

He pulled away and lifted my chin looking into my eyes. "It's just a few more hours until we can go home. Are you going to be okay? I don't want to let you leave if you're not."

I nodded. "Yes. I'll be fine."

"Will you come back up here at five I want to walk down with you and it might take me just a few minutes to finish up but I promise I'm not working late tonight."

Again I nodded. He pulled me close again, his hands fisting in my hair. "Don't walk away from me Drew. I love you. I hope you can see how much I really want you too."

I left his office feeling better about things, but as I neared the stairwell I slowed then stopped. A momentary battle raged inside my head before I turned around and headed straight to Connie's office.

"Hey Connie," I said sticking my head in her door. "I just wanted to ask you who is the woman who stopped in her a few minutes ago."

Connie looked up smiling. "Oh, her name is Carrie. I used to see her around here all the time. I've been surprised to see her here the last couple of evenings."

My heart was suddenly in my throat again. "Oh, okay…thanks."

I took the stairs and went back to my desk. My heart was pounding in my chest. Adam was being dishonest with me. I sat in my desk stewing over the information Connie had given me. Carrie was…the girl that Adam had dated before; the girl that had supposedly dated Ned.

My mind was reeling. No matter how I analyzed it I came to the same conclusion. Adam was having a fling with an old flame. He had her come up the stairs so that I wouldn't see her going to his office. He was staying late to be with her. He came home smelling of the perfume she wore...He was touching her...the perfume was all over his hands.

I couldn't believe it. How had I let this happen again? Was I such a poor judge of character? I just couldn't do this again. Seeing Joe around after he'd gone had left me debilitated, if I had to watch Adam it would destroy me. I wouldn't be able to stay here. I had to leave.

I put my head on my desk and was surprised when I felt someone's hand on my back. It was Amy. She sat down in a chair next to me.

"What's wrong hon?" She asked looking concerned. I tried to fight the tears from coming, but to no avail.

"Amy, do you think that Adam would cheat on me?"

Amy looked surprised. "No I don't." She said emphatically. "Adam loves you. What makes you ask that?"

"Just some things that have been going on, his answers don't add up and I feel like he's hiding something from me. I want so badly to trust him but I'm having a hard time. I can't shake the feeling that I'm going to suddenly be alone again and I'd rather be the one that leaves this time. I don't think I could live through another situation like Joe."

"Listen to me hon." Amy said sternly. "Adam. Is. Not. Joe." She spoke each word separately, punctuated, attempting to drill them into my head. "That man loves you and you need to give him a chance. You know he's been stressed with the new position and I'm sure he can answer any of your questions. Things aren't always as they seem. Don't jump to conclusion hon; give him the opportunity to give you facts before you make a rash decision."

I listened to Amy and she did make sense. I was well known for jumping to conclusions. In the end I conceded. Adam had wanted me to meet him in his office after work and I would. Then I would tell him that I wanted answers. If he couldn't give me answers I was leaving.

My heart was breaking just thinking about it. I wanted answers but I was terrified of what those answers would be. I was terrified that I might be flying back to Austin tomorrow without Adam. At five o'clock I punched the clock and slowly made my way to Adam's office.

He knew something was wrong when he saw my face. Instinctively he came around the desk and stopped in front of me.

"What is it?" He asked. His eyes searched my face but there was nothing but a blank stare. I hid behind a phony mask. I wouldn't allow him to see my pain.

"I know who she is." I said without emotion. "I want answers tonight, real answers or I'll be on a plane tomorrow going home to Austin."

His face contorted with what appeared to be anguish as he moved to close his office door again.

"I'm not letting you do this Drew." He moved to me putting his arms around me but I remained rigid.

"Goddamn you Drew. Can't you see you're breaking my heart? I've given you everything. What more do I need to do?"

My façade was slipping as he held me. I began to tremble then sob.

"Why are you lying and hiding things from me? You want me to trust you…but I can't. I ask questions and the answers don't add up."

"Drew, please baby. I can answer all of your questions tonight, and I will tonight, just don't walk out now… Please."

I sobbed into his chest. I had never hurt so badly in my life. I wanted to believe him. I felt like I would die if I had to walk away. If I survived I would be forever damaged.

He held me for a long time, stroking my back; planting kisses in my hair. When I looked up I could tell he'd been crying too. Taking a tissue from his desk he dried my eyes then kissed the tops of both my cheeks.

"Come on, let's go home." He said wrapping his arm around my waist. "There is something I need to tell you and it can't wait any longer."

We walked out of his office and around the corner to the elevators. Dread began creeping into my mind, twisting my gut as I stood waiting for the elevator. Again the tears threatened to pour from my eyes. What were Adam's answers going to be? Would he confess to a fling with Carrie? Would I be able to move forward with him if he did?

After a minute a small crowd had gathered behind us. I didn't turn around because I didn't want them to see I'd been crying.

"Let's take the stairs." I whispered. "That car is still broken."

"No the car will be here in a minute." He said, pulling me tighter against him.

A moment later, Otis stepped out from the stairwell. He looked at Adam and I thought I saw him nod. Otis took a small metal box from his pocket and Adam pulled me a step closer to the car.

The door of the car opened and I moved to step in then stopped in my tracks. I gasped.

The entire car was filled with red and white cut flowers and roses stacked on shelves that had been placed along the elevator walls. The floor was strewn with rose petals and a crystal chandelier had been temporarily suspended from the ceiling.

I just stood there not quite knowing what to do until Adam pulled me into the car. I looked on in shock as he got down on one knee in front of me. I heard people oohing, saw the flashes of cameras and realized I had an audience. The elevator door wasn't closing, courtesy of Otis and his little metal box.

I caught a whiff of perfume as Adam reached into his pocket and pulled out a ring box. The elevator was filled with the scent he'd had on his hands. I couldn't take my eyes off of him. This man I had fallen completely into.

I cried as he opened the box and asked me to marry him. Cried as I realized the late nights and meetings with Carrie were planning this night for me. Cried because when he was trying to do something wonderful for me I'd been a major bitch to him - and he still loved me.

How fitting, I thought, that he would propose to me in the elevator where it all started. I couldn't think of any place better. All that was missing was the kiss. I couldn't stop myself as I knelt in front of him. He was still waiting for my answer.

"Don't make me suffer baby." He said, his eyes pleading. "Marry me. You know I love you."

"Yes." I said still crying. "Yes Adam Knight. I love you too."

My arms flew around his neck as he pulled me onto his knee. Taking my hand he put the ring on my finger. It fit perfectly and I wondered how he knew what size I wore, but then he knew everything about me.

And then he did it. He'd said he would; said he'd kiss me in front of the whole damn company. I didn't care. I wanted them to see...wanted everyone to know that he was mine.

I heard the applause and the wolf whistles. I saw cameras flashing and I heard Amy yell '*Way to go Ducky.*' And then I was lost in Adam...Falling deeper into Knight.

TWENTY-FIVE

Six months later.....

I stood in the middle of the living room, surveying the empty apartment. Everything was boxed up and loaded onto the moving van that had left just minutes ago. I would be following shortly but I wanted one last look at the home I'd lived in for almost a year. I would miss this place.

If you'd asked me six months ago if I'd live here forever I would have told you I didn't know, but wherever I lived it would be with Adam. I couldn't imagine living life without him.

It's funny how life works. One minute you think you're being flushed down a toilet and the next minute the swirling water has delivered you to the top of the world.

That's what happened six months ago.

Six months ago Adam told me he wanted more. He told me he wanted to get married and start a family. He wanted to build a house on Bainbridge Island and wanted to come home to me every day for the rest of his life.

Six months ago I said yes.

"Are you ready to go babe?" Adam asked, wrapping his arms around my shoulders from behind. I nodded, leaning into the strength of his chest.

We had a lot to do. Next week was the wedding then we'd be off for a month on our honeymoon in Italy.

We'd bought a large piece of property with a tiny house on it. We would live there when we got back until the new house was finished. We were in no hurry.

My entire family was coming into town for the wedding. Daniel was bringing Corinne, Janie was bringing Michael, and Lana was bringing Joe who, by the way, had asked her to marry him. Jules didn't have a boyfriend but I had some thoughts about introducing her to Tom, Adam's younger brother.

Davy was, of course, going to be Adam's Best Man and Amy would be my Maid of honor. Gloria had declined being a bride's maid. She literally had her hands full with the twins, Abigail, and Eva.

Davy had been incredibly shocked that one of them wasn't a boy, but he wasn't disappointed. Gloria had just said she'd known it all along. The two girls were more than enough to keep the couple busy and Gloria's mom had come to stay with them for a while to help out.

The wedding would be a small affair, outside on the property we'd purchased with a gorgeous view of the sound. The weather was quite warm now but the constant ocean breeze would make it bearable.

My dress was light, airy, white gauze; Perfect for the waterfront setting. It was ankle length with spaghetti straps and I'd paired it with some flat, toe sandals. Adam would be wearing white linen drawstring pants with a white linen shirt, un-tucked.

Adam's kiss on my cheek brought me back to the present. I turned in his arms wrapping my own around his waist. I felt so secure and safe here in his arms. I would never doubt him again.

As he'd promised, he told me everything the night he proposed. He'd worked tirelessly getting everything set up from calling Otis out to modify the elevator, to sending out emails ensuring the entire company would be there to witness it. He also hired Carrie.

Carrie was a wedding planner and had some great ideas for decorating the car. When I passed her in the stairwell, she'd been down in the basement all day installing the shelves that would hold all the flowers. She'd also given Adam scent cards for him to select a fragrance for the occasion.

I actually got to meet her and her fiancé, and I got to hear her story first hand. She had gone on a couple of dates with Ned but knew he wasn't for her. She simply stopped seeing him.

She made it clear that Adam had neither stolen her away nor had he broken her heart, but she did think the story was good for a laugh anyway. We'd met the couple for dinner a few times since then and they would be at the wedding.

Jared, Lucy and Paul had all three graduated med school. Lucy and Jared had both accepted internships at a Seattle hospital. Paul however was going to UTMB at Galveston. Amy would be relocating with him back to Texas. I would miss her but at least we could visit when I went to see my parents. It was just a few more hours' drive.

Adam tugged me gently, pulling me toward the door. I let him lead me knowing I would go anywhere as long as I was with him. We turn, taking one last look around then lock the door behind us.

We stop by the office and turn in the key. We give them our forwarding address so they can mail our deposit refund, and then we leave.

Putting on my sunglasses I climb into the seat next to Adam. He cranks the engine then leans across the console, pulling me into a tender kiss. When he releases me he puts the car in drive then twines his fingers through mine, squeezing my hand gently.

"From here on out babe it's me and you." He says smiling down at me.

I return the smile nodding. "Yes baby, me and you." I say as he pulls out onto the main highway.

The rest is history!

Thank you for reading *Falling into Knight.*

Log onto my website @www.ardbook.com to see more books by A.R. Dean. You can also leave reviews @ www.amazon.com/author/ardean

www.ingramcontent.com/pod-product-compliance
Lightning Source LLC
Chambersburg PA
CBHW060152260626
47160CB00001B/234